SPENCER MEETS HIS LADY LOVE

A Seabrook Family Saga, Book Five

CHRISTINE DONOVAN

Sign up for Christine's newsletter to be informed of new releases and to be eligible for special contests and prizes. You can sign up on Christine's website at http://www.christinedonovan.org/

Dear Readers,

I took certain liberties in the time period for the waltz to better suit my story. It became fashionable in Vienna in 1780, but not in England until the Regency period when it was endorsed by Dorothea Lieven, wife of the Russian ambassador. However, to work with my story, I have Spencer and Miranda dancing the waltz in 1806. Any other historical inaccuracies are done on purpose to suit the book.

I hope you enjoy the story!

🏵 Created with Vellum

This book is dedicated to my mother-in-law, Claire Donovan. Never did a more kind, generous and loving soul exist. Thank you for all your support, compassion and understanding over the years. May we have many, many more years to enjoy each other's company.

Thank you to my husband, Michael and my four sons, Shawn, Matt, Danny and Joey. My granddaughter, Olivia, who never fails to make me smile and keeps life real. As always, to my mother, Alberta Murray, my sister, Karen Gomer for always supporting me and being my traveling companions. When is the next trip? To Joanne Smart for being my first reader and encouraging me when writing is hard.

CHAPTER ONE

London 1806

"I'M FINDING IT DIFFICULT DECIDING WHERE TO LOOK," Mr. Stuart Spencer said to his cousin, Lord William Spencer. "All these new debutantes making their formal entrance into society are straining my eyes."

"Unless you want to find yourself leg-shackled, I suggest you look elsewhere. As you very well know, the debutantes and their mamas have one goal in mind. Matrimony."

"It's too bad really, I find the strawberry-blonde standing with Viscount and Viscountess Chambers quite alluring. Must be their one and only daughter if my memory serves me correctly?"

"You will do well and good to stay far away from her. Rumor has it the viscount made some bad investments, is utterly in debt and on the fringe of losing everything back to the crown, including his title. The family is relying on a match that will bring wealth back into their coffers." William cocked a brow. "You, my dear cousin, may not possess a title, but you do have one thing they need—money and plenty of it. Your mother may have wed an untitled gentleman, but our grandfather was an earl and our grandmother a countess. You come from an aristocratic family and best watch yourself with." He nodded in the strawberry-blonde's direction. "That one."

Stuart, called Spencer by most, laughed. "I'll keep all this under advisement," he said with a grin. However, I believe I'll beg an introduction from her father. Excuse me." Spencer didn't need to glance back at his cousin to know he was scowling. And rightfully so. At the tender age of twenty-five, Spencer had no plans to marry anytime soon. He had no business hunting down Lady Miranda Carlton, except he couldn't help himself. While conversing with William he'd been watching Lady Miranda. Her head tilting side to side while carrying on a conversation caused her lovely hair, piled high upon her head, to bob this way and that. The vision had kept his eyes riveted to her. He'd been unable to look elsewhere. The white gown she wore made her skin appear iridescent in the flickering light from the chandeliers. Unfortunately, he could not make out her eye color from this distance, nor could he tell if her face was smattered with freckles as most strawberry-blondes were. But he would soon. His long strides ate up the distance between them until he finally arrived beside the Carlton family.

"Viscount, Viscountess." Spencer bowed. "It is a pleasure to see you again." If the viscount and viscountess appeared shocked at his words, they hid it well. Although they traveled in the same privileged circles, he'd never been formally introduced or spoken a word to either of them. He only hoped they knew his name.

"Mr. Spencer," the viscount said with a knowing look. Spencer should have known he would have done research on the available gentlemen of the *ton* before introducing their daughter to society. No doubt, only the richest graced their suitable marriage list for their only daughter. Was he on it? *Doesn't matter. I'm not looking for a wife.*

"May I present my daughter, Lady Miranda. Lady Miranda, this is Mr. Stuart Spencer, the grandson of the Dowager Countess of Bridgeton and the late Fifth Earl of Bridgeton."

Miranda curtsied. "It is a pleasure to make your acquaintance, Mr. Spencer."

Spencer bowed while taking her hand and bringing it to his lips. "The pleasure is all mine." He removed his hand quickly, not wanting to give her father any cause to think their search for a suitor was over. Spencer merely wanted to meet Lady Miranda and dance a waltz with her. Not spend the rest of his life as her husband.

Although, as he held her small, gloved hand in his and peered into her emerald green eyes, and noticed the light dusting of freckles on her pink cheeks, something shifted inside him. Something subtle and elusive, but something nonetheless. He would worry about the significance of that later. For the time being he would wait patiently for the first waltz as Lady Miranda promised it to him.

Begging his leave, he sought out liquid refreshments from a passing waiter and didn't see his cousin sneak up on him.

"So, you met her. What do you think?" William asked with a shake of his head and a glare in his eyes. Almost as though he knew...something. But what?

Spencer downed his bubbly in one swallow, regretting it immediately as the fuzz made a comeback up his throat and nose making them tingle and him unable to speak. After a minute, he cleared his throat and replied, "Yes."

"Yes. That is all you have to say." William huffed. "I, cousin, watched from across the room and saw your eyes light up as you bowed, most gallantly, before her. And just now, as I approached you, you were lost in your own mind and had a lovesick look on your face. You didn't even see me approach. Shall we go and find Grandmother and tell her the good news?"

"What?" Spencer could hardly breathe all of a sudden. "Me, getting married? Are you out of your bloody mind?" he yelled then cringed when several people glared their way. "It's a waltz, nothing more, nothing less."

"If you say so," William said with a half grin. "Go have your waltz, I'm going to find the gaming tables and relieve someone of his precious coin."

As William walked away and Spencer contemplated joining him at the tables, he realized his dance with Miranda was about to begin. He made his way back around the ball-room and bowed before her.

"Lady Miranda, I believe this is my dance."

"So it is."

She placed her tiny hand on his arm, paused, frowned at him and then allowed herself to be escorted onto the dance floor. So she had also felt the scorching heat they created when they touched? Good to know he was not alone on that front.

As he held Miranda in his arms, perfect form and distance between their bodies, he wished his insides would stop burning. He could hardly take his eyes off her beautiful face. Her eyes were a deep emerald green encased in long lashes. Her red-blonde hair, carefully piled high on her head with several curls cascading down her back promised to be silky and smooth to his touch. Unlike the so-called perfect English Lady, she had a smattering of freckles across her nose and high on her cheekbones. It only added to her allure in Spencer's mind. She stood tall and willowy thin, not the highly sought after curvy and voluptuous. Only waltzing with her now, gave him imminent knowledge that she indeed had curves in all the right places. Her bosom pushed against her bodice, giving him a sneak peek of its creamy goodness.

"Mr. Spencer, are you unwell?"

"Pardon?"

The concern in her eyes was touching—albeit unnecessary.

"You groaned. I thought, perhaps, you were distressed."

"Distressed?" He was distressed all right, but not for the reason she would guess. If he didn't concentrate on something other than the delectable lady he was dancing with, the entire ballroom full of people would see what was happening to the lower half of his body.

"Forgive me, Lady Miranda, I am fine. Just in awe of your beauty and grace."

"Thank you, Mr. Spencer." Her brows drew together in the cutest way, then relaxed. "You are very light on your feet for a gentleman and quite graceful as well."

He laughed. He couldn't help himself which caused her cheeks to turn a most becoming shade of pink. "Indeed. It is because my grandmother not only insisted that my cousins and I take dance lessons, which all gentlemen take, but she also tested us until she was satisfied with our abilities. I fear she thought we would embarrass her. "

"How wonderful to have a grandmother take such interest in you. Pray tell, who are your cousins? Perhaps I would like to dance with them as well, knowing I would be in capable hands. The slippers I wear on my feet give me no protection from a man's foot, and I so value my feet."

Spencer chuckled at her words. "The Earl of Bridgeton and his brother, Lord William Spencer."

"Are your cousins married?" she asked, then paused, her eyes widening. "Oh, dear. I have offended you. I am truly sorry."

Spencer's heart sank at her words. He must learn to hide his emotions better around her. No doubt she had read his disappointment. "No offense taken. The Earl is married to Sir Phillip Trenton's sister, Lady Katherine. William is presently unattached and according to him, he will remain so for the foreseeable future."

"I see."

"Do you?" He lowered his head and murmured close to her ear, and he heard her inhale right before her body quivered in his arms. "Don't waste your time trying to snare William into matrimony. He will not relent to you or any other female in this room."

"Why not? Does he prefer men?"

Spencer missed a step, and they nearly collided with Lord and Lady Northborough.

"Aren't you a little young to know about things such as that?"

This time when she blushed it wasn't just her cheeks that turned red. Her neck and the tops of her breasts flushed as well, and Spencer swallowed the moan trying to escape his throat.

"I heard the servants talking one night. Is it true? Can men sleep with men?"

Once again he almost collided with the Northborough's who sent concerned looks his way. He smiled and mouthed an apology. Thank God it was someone like the Northborough's. If he'd done, to other members of the *ton* what he'd just done to them twice, they would have given him a tongue lashing and caused a scene. How did he know? Once, last season, a young couple danced a waltz and one of them tripped, he did not know which, the lady or the gentleman, not that it mattered. What mattered was old Lord Easton danced with his new, young bride. He took offense and lashed out and embarrassed the young couple. The lady in question, ran in tears seeking the shelter of her mother's arms while the young man stood on the ballroom floor looking mortified. Eventually, his brother came to his rescue. It was all the gossips talked about until the next member of the *ton* caused a scandal and became the object of the gossips' desires. Spencer didn't relish being on the receiving end of the gossips. It could ruin one's reputation and life.

"Lady Miranda," before he could come up with a suitable answer, the music ended and he escorted her back to her parents and bowed off. While casually walking away, he looked over his shoulder once to see Miranda gazing back at him. He nodded his head and went in search of William.

AS MIRANDA WATCHED the handsome Mr. Spencer stroll away from her, she inwardly cringed. Once again her mouth landed her in a pickle. When he'd begged an introduction from her parents, she'd been thrilled. She may have never met Mr. Spencer before, but his reputation was well known to her. But not for the reasons one would think.

Her mother confided in her that they were in desperate need for funds. They'd gone into even more debt to purchase gowns for this season—her very first Season. And according to her parents, with any luck, her last.

Before coming here tonight her mother had gone over a list of eligible and suitable gentlemen whom they wanted her to consider. All rich and from well-connected families. Mr. Spencer and his cousin's name were on the list.

At the time, she didn't think much about the list. Several men whose names graced it she'd already met, and she truly hoped to never find herself betrothed to them. And if she did, she would run away rather than summit to being a wife to any of them. Deep down inside she resented the fact that she had to snare a husband quickly to appease her parents. And truthfully, how did her marrying a rich man help them? Didn't it usually work the other way around when the gentleman received his intended's dowry?

Oh dear! Did she still have a dowry? Not that it mattered when it came to Mr. Spencer. No doubt she frightened him off with her shocking words. If she ever had the privilege of dancing with him again she would apologize and then stitch her lips together. Never utter another inappropriate word or ask a shocking question.

Her parents always said her mouth would be her undoing. Now she understood. Think before you speak had been drilled into her from an early age. How had she forgotten tonight with Mr. Spencer? Easily, she'd found him fascinating and utterly handsome and when she became nervous she forgot that important lesson.

From the moment she spied him, walking across the room, his eyes on her, she knew her life would never be the same. Mayhap, not because she would eventually marry the man. Because, for the first time in her seventeen years, her insides awoke and sizzled at the very idea of being with a man. Even if she didn't know what being with a man meant? She wanted it. With him. With Mr. Stuart Spencer.

Sadly though, she didn't believe he would marry someone like her. Someone who couldn't hold her tongue, and she mentally crossed his name off her list as well as his cousins. Another reason to cross them off came down to age. Most wealthy gentlemen didn't marry until at least thirty and they were but twenty-five. Who was left? Three men reputed to be rogues of the worst kind. Lord Thomas Seabrook, eldest son of a duke, Baron Norwich, only son of an earl and Lord Edward Worthington, only son of an Marquess. Rakehells of the foulest kind.

As of yet, she'd not had the fortune or misfortune of

making their acquaintance. Not to mention, all three of them were hardly twenty. Not exactly the age men considered marriage.

No, they were crossed off her list as well while they sowed their wild oats, gambling, drinking, and whoring.

At least she didn't say any of that out loud. She had an addiction to gothic novels which fueled her unladylike thoughts. Thoughts she could keep to herself, her speech was another thing entirely.

Too bad her mouth escaped her control. She rather liked Mr. Spencer. He didn't dress like a dandy, which she preferred. In her mind, how could she take a gentleman seriously when he wore a salmon or chartreuse colored greatcoat, waistcoat, or breeches? No. She'd learned long ago dandies were not to her taste. Handsome looks were an asset, but not something she needed in a husband. Kindness was a necessity as patience and a sense of humor were as well. Because she spoke her mind before thinking, a sense of humor topped her list. Money and wealth might top her parents' list, but if she wanted a nice, happy life, her husband must laugh and laugh aplenty. Or at least laugh with her when she made a faux pas. Which to the horror of her parents, she did often.

As her thoughts drift back to Mr. Spencer, she had to admit he was most handsome with his dark hair and bluish-green eyes. At times they appeared green and other times blue. How odd, yet she'd found them mesmerizing.

She spoke the truth when she told him he danced gracefully. He did indeed. They were well matched in that respect since she could admit to herself she was indeed a fine dancer. More than fine, quite competent as was he.

His voice, a deep baritone, caused her skin to tingle in a good way, not like nails on a board in the schoolroom.

Too bad she ruined what they might have had with talk about men sleeping with men. She saw the blood drain from his face at her words. No doubt if the waltz hadn't concluded when it had, he would have bowed off, embarrassing her and her parents. Oh well, nothing to do about that now. It was in the past. As was Mr. Spencer.

"Miranda," her mother's voice interrupted her musings, "Please let me see your dance card. It should be full with names by now."

She reluctantly handed it over.

"Tsk, tsk, this will not do. Come with me while I introduce you to the gentlemen on our list. We can't have you sitting out dances, you will get the reputation of a wallflower. And no daughter of mine will be reduced to wallflower status."

"Yes, Mother." She sighed as she wondered if she could somehow break her leg, *now*, rescuing her from those *men* on the *list*.

The next hour passed in a blur of introductions and dances with strangers. Several of whom had horrible breath and sweaty hands even through their gloves and hers. And most of these men were not on the *list*. Torture, it was pure torture to keep a smile plastered on her face and partake in polite conversation. A time or two she shocked her partner with her candid words. One gentleman blushed profusely. *Really? Am I that horrid and embarrassing when I speak my mind?*

Once, she found herself dancing a waltz with Lord Thomas Seabrook, who practically ignored her and if she wasn't mistaken appeared to be in his cups. Oh, he was handsome, and debonair, but not for her. He wasn't even out of university. Why her mother had his name on the list was crazy.

And contrary to what her mother suggested, she would not try to ensnare any man into marrying her. He either wanted to marry her or he didn't. Simple as that.

Besides, she could not, in good conscious, compromise

herself for the sake of her parents, nor would she do that to anyone else. Why should they suffer because of her father's bad judgment when it came to managing his finances?

Oh, she knew entrapments happened and often. But not to her. She could never forgive herself for deceiving someone. For luring him out into the gardens on a warm, dark night such as this. Letting herself be caught with her lips on his, or worse, his hand on her bosom. In her mind, the lips she kissed belonged to Stuart Spencer. Her arms went around her waist as she shivered in awareness. Awareness of what, she wanted to know.

Not far from where she stood now, near the refreshment table, a deep voice drifted her way enhancing her already over-aware senses. Mr. Spencer was in deep conversation with his cousin, she presumed the man to be his cousin as they resembled each other. She could only surmise as she had yet to be introduced to him. An oversight on her mother's part, no doubt.

Plucking a cup of punch off the table, very carefully so as not to get a drop of the pink liquid on the fingertips of her pure white gloves, she sipped it while pretending to listen to her closest friend Lady Beatrice Stone prattle on and on about dancing twice with Lord Frances Herman. A bore of a man in her opinion, not that Beatrice cared about her or anyone else's opinion. She looked smitten with the bore.

"Beatrice, surely you are not setting your sights on Lord Frances already?"

Her friend blushed which answered the question. "Why not. He is handsome and witty. Why I nearly peed myself laughing while we waltzed."

"No reason. The Season is just beginning, you don't want to find yourself betrothed so soon you miss the rest of it." Surely her friend wasn't in love already? Love at first sight? *Please*, some people were so gullible to believe in such a farce.

"Is not the point of a Season to find a husband?"

Sometimes Miranda wondered how she and Beatrice ever became friends. They couldn't be more different. Perhaps that's why the friendship worked so well.

"I believe you are right. And if Lord Frances is who you want, then I'm happy for you."

Beatrice leaned close to her ear and whispered, "I see who has caught your eye and he is most handsome."

Miranda blinked and to her horror, blushed.

"Did you think I didn't notice you waltzing with Mr. Spencer? Nor the way you were just eyeing him like candy the whole time I was talking to you. Which was so rude, did you even hear a thing I said?"

No...I mean yes...sorry." She should have known. She'd never been able to keep secrets from Beatrice. Lowering her voice she said, "He is very handsome and appears nice enough."

"But..."

"But, you know me. I may have said a thing or two that shocked him during that most scandalous dance called a waltz. Which I cannot believe my parents let me participate in. Most debutantes are not allowed to waltz. It's unseemly intimate."

Beatrice shook her head and frowned. "You might as well tell me what you said? I'll find out sooner or later."

"You don't want to know."

"That horrible?"

"Well, I shocked even myself after I uttered the words. And I'm quite convinced Mr. Spencer was too. Because really, how could he not when I asked if his cousin, William, preferred the company of men."

Beatrice gasped and covered her mouth. A confused expression crossed her face. "I don't understand?"

Good, Miranda thought.

CHAPTER TWO

"WHO DO YOU KEEP LOOKING AT?" QUESTIONED WILLIAM.

"What...who...I don't know what you mean."

"Oh come now Spencer, I know you too well. And if I had to guess I would say Lady Miranda Carlton has caught your eye."

He smiled as he remembered the inappropriate conversation they had during their dance. "She is lovely, if a bit unconventional. Speaks her mind which is refreshing, but I best stay clear. She has set her sights on marriage." Too bad really because he would like to get to know her better.

William laughed. "Don't they all."

"Have Geoffrey and Katherine arrived yet? They are awfully late."

Spencer felt bad for causing the scowl on his cousin's face. Poor William. Caught in so many secrets and lies. Secrets Spencer knew, not that he was ever told, but he put it all together not long ago.

"They are not attending. Got a missive from Geoffrey right before we left explaining Katherine was feeling under the weather, which was a lie no doubt."

"Why didn't you tell me?"

"Just because we live in the same house doesn't mean I have to tell you everything."

"Sorry." Spencer, wanting to escape his family, but not interested in renting rooms where all the other bachelors of the *ton* resided, moved in with William into one of his family's Mayfair homes right down the street from Spencer's.

"Sorry. None of my business."

"Correct."

"Anyway, I suppose you could do worse than Lady Miranda. She is comely and her teeth are white and straight."

"You noticed?" Spencer was shocked.

"Yes, well," he shrugged his shoulders, "not until you seemed interested in her."

"I haven't made up my mind about interested or not. She has her sights on marriage, and I'm not convinced I want to give up my degenerate ways just yet." Damn it all. If only she didn't need to marry soon. Getting to know her would be a welcome surprise.

William laughed. "You are such a reprobate and a rakehell. Do you think you can change?"

"Funny. If you could, then I certainly can."

"Who says I changed my ways?"

Spencer ignored the question. He didn't want to get into all the secrets that surrounded William, Geoffrey, and Katherine. But what secrets of theirs he did know were safe with him.

SPENCER HAD a lapse of sanity the following morning and not only sent flowers to Carlton house but also arrived for tea during afternoon visiting hours.

Led into a drawing room on the second floor, the butler announced him.

"Mr. Stuart Spencer."

He took a seat in a vacant chair facing a settee where Lady Miranda and her mother resided. One other chair was occupied by the elderly Lord Templeton. Surely he was not in the market for a wife? Worse yet, would Miranda's parents consider him. He was worth a small fortune and would undoubtedly die soon, leaving Miranda a wealthy widow.

"Lady Miranda, Viscountess, thank you for receiving me. What lovely weather we are having today."

"Not that lovely," mumbled Lord Templeton, "my rheumatism is acting up, rain is coming."

Did the man know that would not help his cause any? He sat, hunched over, clutching his walking stick. His eyes were bloodshot, his skin puffy and bluish in color. Clearly the man had indulged in more than his share of spirits during his lifetime. His long lifetime at that.

"Yes, well, it is lovely now," replied Lady Miranda. "Mother and I plan to take a carriage ride in the park later, so I hope the rain holds off."

"I think it will." Damn, how could Spencer have forgotten how much he hated calling on a lady? He was no good at small talk. The weather, who cared about the weather except for the elderly like Lord Templeton with his rheumatism.

What he wanted was to spend time with Lady Miranda. The real Lady Miranda. Not the impostor sitting prim and proper before him. Not that she wasn't prim and proper, she was, it's just she was more than that. He could admit today, after being shocked by her words last night, that she was a breath of fresh air with her candid and honest words.

Of course, her parents would be shocked at what she said to him. But he wouldn't mind learning more about these unconventional things she knew about even if they were a little too close to home for comfort.

"As I was saying, Mr. Spencer," said the viscountess, interrupting his thoughts, "I didn't see your mother or grandmother last evening. Are they in the country?"

"Grandmother no. She attended last evening, although she left quite early. My mother and my younger sisters are in the country for some fresh air."

"Are they not attending the Season then?" Miranda asked.

"No. My sisters are young. Only six and seven. It'll be a while before they make their come out."

"I didn't realized they were so much younger than you," the viscountess said."

"Yes, well." He shrugged his shoulders. "They are." Spencer never really thought about the years in between his birth and those of his sisters. Obviously, his mother had trouble conceiving after him. It was after the birth of his younger sister, Elizabeth that their father died from consumption. The loss still pained his heart. His father had been larger than life to him. And ever since his death their mother had wallowed away in her grief and invented ailments. Thank God for their grandmother who basically raised his sisters.

Shortly after, he took his leave and found himself walking into White's to a loud commotion. The hairs on the back of his neck rose as he recognized the voices of Sir Phillip Trenton, Geoffrey, and William arguing long before he caught sight of them.

"What is going on," he said as he stepped up to the three men standing close together. Sir Phillip had murder in his eyes. Spencer never did like the chap. He had beady, shifty eyes that made one uncomfortable. Made one wonder what lurked inside his mind.

Sir Phillip turned his way piercing Spencer with those

murderous dark eyes. "These two are keeping me from seeing my sister."

"I beg your pardon, but as I understand it, Lady Katherine doesn't want to see you," Spencer said with conviction."

Both cousins looked his way, shocked. "How do you know?" Geoffrey asked.

"She told me."

"She did?" This from William and Sir Phillip simultaneously.

"Yes. Now if you don't want the whole of the *ton* to know about your *personal* differences, I suggest you end this conversation. They probably already have the betting books out and money being put down on the outcome. Not that there will be an outcome, as I believe, Sir Phillip was just leaving."

Spencer hated when he had to get in the middle of his cousins and Sir Phillip. Especially since he only could speculate on the dissention between the three. It would be much easier if he knew the whole story.

After Trenton left, Spencer gestured to a group of chairs facing the hearth. Once seated, he motioned to a server for drinks. Glass in hand, he downed it in one swallow. "What the bloody hell were you two thinking?"

"He started it," William said with a frown. "He wouldn't shut up about Katherine. She doesn't ever want to see him."

"He is a moron. A money grubbing moron," Geoffrey said into his still full brandy. He placed it on a side table and rose. "I'm going home."

"Is Trenton becoming a bother?" Spencer asked William once Geoffrey was gone. Clearly he was if the altercation he just happened upon was any indication. Had there been other instances he didn't know about? He also wanted to know if William, Geoffrey, and Katherine were taking great pains to keep their secret affairs just that—secret. If knowledge came out…Spencer cringed at the thought. Three people's lives would be ruined beyond repair. Not to mention, what this would do to their grandmother? Spencer didn't believe she would survive the scandal.

William shrugged his shoulders. "Nothing we can't handle." He held his glass up. "Another round." He mouthed to the server. "So please tell me you didn't call upon the lovely Lady Miranda this afternoon?"

Spencer's mouth dropped. "How did you know?"

"We do live in the same house. Besides, the butler informed me. Are you out of your bloody mind? Never mind. Don't answer that because I know you are."

"If anyone is out of his mind it is you." Did William have any idea he played with fire with the risk of incineration.

"Me?"

"You know what I'm talking about. But as for me, I haven't met a lady who intrigues me as she does. She speaks her mind and doesn't appear to play games. It's refreshing."

"Just don't find yourself alone with her in a dark corner, or in a deserted room, or out on a dimly lit terrace, or in a poorly lit garden, the list goes on and on. Because if you do, you'll find yourself with a fiancée."

"Would that be so bad?"

"Are you daft?"

Was he? He didn't think so. Just tired of life as it was. He didn't want a wife just yet. But he did want Miranda. In every way possible known to man. He'd already acknowledged he wanted to get to know her better. Now he admitted to wanting more. He wanted to possess her mind, body, and soul.

"PLEASE, CLAUDIA," Miranda said. "Hurry up already, Mother

must be waiting and I don't want to arrive late for my first night at Almack's. I've waited a lifetime for this night to come." And she had. Ever since she'd been a little girl her mother talked about her time at Almack's. How it was where she met her father and knew instantly she would marry him. Miranda didn't believe in love at first sight, but she always dreamed of Almack's and her very own knight in shining armor. Tonight she would see firsthand if the famed club lived up to its reputation.

"Oh, milady," Claudia said as she placed the last cream flower in her hair. "You look beautiful. You will probably get three marriage proposals tonight alone."

Miranda's heartbeat increased. "Oh, how exciting that would be. But truly, I'm not ready to get betrothed until the end of the Season. I don't want to miss out on anything." Did she just utter the words, *how exciting that would be?* No. It. Would. Not. Be. Her father would make her accept the first one that came in, and she didn't believe Spencer would be offering any marriage proposals. She didn't want to get married until she had time to get to know him. Something about him made her eager to be in his company. And there was so much more if she admitted it to herself. Last night she'd dreamed of a mysterious man who kissed her and made her feel wonderful and free. Free from her parents' strict rules. Free from her mother's nagging to sit up straight, be a lady, and think before you speak. Oh, she loved her mother dearly, but she needn't remind her so often. It made Miranda feel lacking somehow.

Now, as they sat in their carriage, it was no less. Her mother ticked off all the things she need do and must not do. Did the woman have any idea how it twisted up her insides until it confused her? She quite possibly might mix up the do's and don'ts.

Arriving at Almack's took longer than Miranda thought

possible. She could barely sit still in the coach as they waited to disembark before the long stairs that would take them into the famous establishment.

Once inside, she could hardly believe all the young debutants, such as herself, milling around smiling, laughing, and gossiping. Where were all the gentlemen? Oh there were men around, but not nearly in the numbers she had thought. Perhaps it was early in the evening and they came later after visiting their clubs. Yes. That must be it.

Which had her wondering if a certain Mr. Spencer would attend this evening. She would be beyond disappointed if he did not have a membership. But of course he had one. What upstanding gentleman of the *ton* didn't? But just because he had a subscription didn't mean he attended on a regular basis.

Just as she helped herself to some watered down punch she saw Beatrice stroll her way, her lovely white gown billowing around her legs. Her friend was tall like her, but where Miranda was thin, Beatrice was curvy and plump in all the right places. Pretty as a picture with her dark hair, blue eyes, and creamy white skin. Ever since they were young, Miranda noticed men leering at her friend. It always made her uncomfortable, but not Beatrice who had older sisters and was used to being around young gentlemen.

"Can you believe we are finally attending Almack's? My twin sisters did nothing but tease me when they had their first Season. Now they are fat." She giggled. "Fatter than I and married with babies drooling over them. Now who is having all the fun? We are and they have to keep house, submit to their husbands in bed, and..." She paused and tapped Miranda's arm with her fan. "Are you listening to me?"

"Look who just came in the door?" Miranda whispered as her heart began to pound furiously. Oh my. How handsome he looked this evening dressed in black formalwear. When he handed his hat and cape to the doorman his tussled hair made her sigh.

"Who?" Beatrice squinted toward the entrance.

"Would you put your spectacles on? You're liable to trip and stumble into someone. Please sit down with me. I don't want to look too eager." They moved to a row of chairs and sat down.

"Perhaps that wouldn't be such a bad idea if I found a certain gentleman who interested me."

"Beatrice," she admonished. "How can you say that? Besides, what about Lord Herman? Have you fallen out of love so quickly?"

She looked thoughtful. "Perhaps. Anyway, take your Mr. Spencer." She batted her eyelashes. "Tell me you would not purposely bump into him to get his attention?"

Would she? "Beatrice, I would do no such thing. Quiet. Here he comes." The roar of her blood rushing in her ears was deafening.

"Lady Miranda," Mr. Spencer said as he bowed over her hand and held it a tad too long. Molten heat spread up her arm and settled deep inside her belly. "It is a pleasure to see you again so soon." Then he turned to Beatrice and hit her with a dazzling smile. Was no one safe from his charms? Miranda thought.

"Mr. Stuart Spencer, may I present, Lady Beatrice Stone."

Once again he bowed, this time over Beatrice's white-gloved hand, but Miranda noticed he dropped hers quickly. "How lovely to make your acquaintance. Are you ladies enjoying Almack's?"

Before she could say a word her friend began. "Yes. It is just as I imagined it would be. When I was a young girl my sisters used to go on and on about here, and I was dreadfully jealous."

"I remember your twin sisters well. They are both

married, are they not?"

"Yes and fat."

"Beatrice," Miranda scolded. "Mr. Spencer does not need to know such things."

"Indeed not," he said with a mischievous twinkle in his eyes. "They broke hearts all over London when they wed."

"Oh, I doubt that," Beatrice said with a frown as she stood up. "Although I could be wrong. Excuse me, Miranda, Mr. Spencer."

"I'm sorry for Beatrice, she tends to speak before thinking." At the knowing look he sent her, heat scorched her cheeks and she blurted out, "I know what you're thinking?"

"Is this seat taken?"

"No."

Spencer sat in the seat vacated by Lady Beatrice. He leaned close to her ear, and she held her breath as he whispered, "Tell me what I'm thinking?"

"That I do the same thing," she said on an exhale while his warm breath caressed her ear deliciously.

The sound of his laughter warmed her insides. "I would never be so forward as to insinuate such a thing even if it were true."

"You were thinking it, though." No matter what he said, she wouldn't be fooled. He had been thinking it.

"Perhaps we could find a more intimate corner to continue this fascinating conversation." The twinkle in his eyes and his carefree expression had her insides churning with something she could not explain. It was uncomfortable and pleasant all at the same time.

He stood, his arm out, waiting for her to accept his escort. *Should I?* She stood and placed her hand on his offered arm, prepared this time for the heat that burned her palm, traveled up her arm, and curled around her heart. Before she knew it the sneaky devil had escorted her to a quiet corner and two vacant chairs. If her mother found her in such a cozy, intimate setting, God only knew what she'd do. Force Mr. Spencer to ask for her hand. She frowned. She would never want him to be forced to do something he didn't want too. She never wanted to be the person who took his carefree existence from him.

After she sat and rearranged her skirts she allowed herself to look at him, really look at him, and her heart stopped at the intense way he stared at her. He looked at her as though his eyes were trying to peek into her soul. Penetrate inside and find all her hidden secrets. Did she even have hidden secrets? Not that she minded his attention, but at that moment his eyes were an intense dark blue color and she found herself lost into the depths of them. She shook her head to clear her befuddled mind.

"Stop looking at me like that?" Oh dear, it came out a little more forceful than she intended.

He blinked, leaned back in his chair, and smiled. "Sorry. Not my intention to make you nervous."

"You didn't."

"No? I'm disappointed." He winked. "I must be losing my touch."

"You like to make young ladies nervous?" Her heart stilled. Mayhap he was not the kind person she thought.

"Truthfully, I don't. I do, however, like teasing you. I've no idea why, except to say it is refreshing to have a conversation with someone about something besides the weather. Don't you think it's a pointless and ridiculous subject to talk about? Because really, who cares about the weather. Especially in London when most days are cool and rainy."

She fought the urge to giggle. "Mr. Spencer, I believe you just made my first conversation about the weather interesting and amusing. What else can we talk about?"

His smile, totally and completely focused on her, made

her insides melt. "We could discuss gloves and why we must wear them? He glanced around the room, then reached for one of her gloved hands and held it in his. Turning it over, he made small circles on her palm with his index finger, and she sighed at the sensations invading her body. Moisture pooled between her legs and she feared she'd relieved herself a little. How mortifying.

"Would it be scandalous if lords and lady's touched, skin to skin? I think not. And what about corsets, a lady should be able to breathe and eat. Besides, would it be so improper for a gentleman, such as myself, to wrap his arms around his lady friend's waist and actually feel her body beneath his sensitive hands?" More moisture. Perhaps she should excuse herself and visit the water closet. But before she could utter a word, he spoke again. "Or neck clothes? A gentleman can hardly breathe when it's tied correctly. Can't be good for the brain or lungs. Not only that, when a lady wraps her arms around his neck, its cuts off his air even more. What is more important than air you ask? The feel of a lady's warm hands touching the sensitive skin surrounding his neck. Hence, why cravats are expendable."

Miranda couldn't help herself this time and she giggled. She covered her mouth with her gloved hand as several old matrons looked disapprovingly her way. So much for thinking their cozy corner gave them privacy.

"I believe my mother would be shocked to hear our conversation. Perhaps we should discuss something a little less scandalous." Not that she wanted to change the topic. This one entertained her and made her feel wicked. Mr. Spencer was a bad influence. She managed to get herself into trouble all on her own, she didn't need someone else helping her. But try as she might, she could not move. If Almack's burned down to the ground around her and Spencer, she would stay as long as he did.

"Indeed." He wiggled his brows up and down, and she bit her lower lip to stop from laughing. "What pray tell should we talk about now?"

She leaned slightly toward him and lowered her voice. "Tell me about gentlemen's clubs. What do you do there? Do men flaunt their mistresses in scandalous clothing? Do men get into their cups and fall down? Are fortunes lost and made in card games? It's unfair that it's all a secret from the female class. We have nothing more exciting than our sewing circles."

"If I confide in you, I might get my membership revoked." He touched her hand with his and squeezed, sending sparks shooting up her arm. "But I can tell you this, it is not as exciting as you think. Married men I think, attend so they can loosen their neck cloths, use foul language, and drink and gamble to their hearts content without being harassed by their wives. Single men enjoy a reprieve from marriage-minded mamas and their daughters."

"Oh." Her heart dropped inside her chest. Is that how he saw her? Then she lowered her eyes and couldn't look away from his large gloved hand, covering her smaller one, feeling decadent and improper. When he pulled away she frowned and shivered as all the warmth left her body.

"Forgive me," Spencer said as he looked around. "I should not have been so forward as to touch you." He stood and bowed. "I see my cousin trying to get my attention. I bid you farewell." He turned, then pivoted back, his eyes focused once again solely on her. "May I call on you tomorrow afternoon?"

It took all her resolve not to draw attention to herself by standing and twirling around with joy. Instead she nodded her head and smiled. "Yes. I would like that very much, Mr. Spencer."

"Until tomorrow then."

Her eyes followed his every move until he was around the corner and most certainly out the door. Never in all her life had she seen such a handsome man who was also interesting and funny. Sometimes she found herself nervous around him and other times she forgot herself and enjoyed his company. Probably more than she should. Her eyes scanned the room and wondered if anyone saw him holding her hand?

What if her mother saw? She inhaled and exhaled. If her mother witnessed it, she would have marched over and made her leave. Placing her hand over her heart she wondered when it would slow. Mr. Spencer made her heart pound and she never wanted the feeling to end. He did other things to her body she didn't understand, but she hoped to in the near future. With him, of course. As her eyes scanned the other gentlemen in the room, and she compared them to Spencer, they all fell lacking. Not only in looks, but in presence. His presence commanded her attention and his penetrating eyes held her captured.

"I WAS THINKING we could stay a tad longer," Spencer remarked as he approached William. He was breaking all his own rules by spending time alone with one woman, but he couldn't help himself. Lady Miranda was like a breath of fresh air. Not ruled by strict social etiquette or by her mama. Something not easily found in London. And when you did, it was to be enjoyed and cherished.

"Are you out of your bloody mind? Almack's is an eligible gentleman's nightmare unless one wants to get hooked by the parson's noose. For those wishing to stay single, such as myself, I prefer other more gentlemanly pursuits. A place where a man can get a real drink, not watered down punch and soft biscuits."

"I believe you have me there. If Almack's really wants to attract more eligible members of the *ton,* they should serve spirits. Then again, a man in his cups is more likely to find himself in a precarious situation where the word betrothed is attached to his name." He shivered at the thought. If he'd been under the influence of whiskey or brandy, no telling what he might have said or done to Miranda. Not that he worried he would do something bad to her, even in his cups, Spencer was good-natured. Unlike some men who got downright mean. The only thing he may have done was lead her to a dark corner or behind a potted plant and capture her lips with his. All evening long, he found his eyes drawn back again and again to her pink, lush, full lips. When she'd caught her front teeth on her bottom lip he'd almost groaned out loud. Actually, now that he had time to think about things, perhaps it was time to leave. Because if he stayed he might just give in to his desires, grab her and duck behind the privacy of a potted plant. Though in reality, the plant didn't truly hide them completely enough from prying eyes. It was all an illusion.

Laughing, William pulled him out of his contemplations and it was good to hear and see his cousin enjoying himself. Ever since Geoffrey and Katherine's wedding, William had taken on a stiff demeanor. Come to think of it, Geoffrey hadn't laughed or been carefree in a longtime either. And Katherine, beautiful, kind, and loving Katherine, always watching the two men in her life with a troubled frown. Oh what a tangled web his cousins lived in. He wouldn't trade places with either of them for all the crown jewels.

"You have this odd look on your face." William took his cloak and hat from the doorman. "Ever since you met Lady Miranda Carlton you've been acting strange. And I mean strange in *not* a good way."

"You are jealous because you haven't a single lady to flirt

with." The moment the words escaped his mouth, and he witnessed the shock on William's face, he wished he could take them back. "Sorry. I know it's none of my business, but perhaps if you met someone you could..."

"Give it a rest. My life is just as I want it to be."

Spencer didn't believe him. If William's life was as he wanted it to be, he would be married to Katherine. Katherine would, most certainly, not be married to Geoffrey. And Geoffrey would be free to pursue other manly pursuits.

Once they left Almack's they settled on a visit to Brooks and found the place quiet which suited Spencer perfectly. While William took a seat to play Faro, he settled in front of the fireplace and sipped a fine brandy.

As his eyes were riveted to the red, orange, and yellow flames leaping from the logs, his mind ran wild with thoughts of Miranda and how he had nearly leaned into her and kissed her earlier that evening. In front of half the members of the *ton* and the Patrons of Almack's themselves. His membership would have been revoked on the spot, and he would be banned for life. *Not really such a terrible thing.*

Against his better judgment, he'd wanted desperately to take her into his arms and teach her about the delicious art of kissing. Because he didn't believe for a moment, she'd ever been kissed before. Heat raced through his veins at the vision of her leaning into him, her full pink lips slightly parted, her eyes closed as she waited for him.

"For Christ sake, get a grip." He scrubbed his hands down his face.

"Talking to yourself, cousin?"

Spencer didn't have to look to know it was Geoffrey speaking to him.

"Geoffrey. Have a seat. What brings you to Brooks this fine evening?"

"Fine evening? Have you looked outside recently? It

started pouring about half ten. My driver could no longer see so I suggested we stop here."

When one looked at Geoffrey, all anyone saw was a handsome, debonair earl. A loving husband and brother. If anyone bothered to look closely, which most members of the *ton* didn't, would they see what Spencer saw? A tormented man battling his inner demons because he was different. Different because he did not like women. Oh, he liked women well enough, just not enough to bed them. Spencer sighed, it was good most people didn't pay close attention to Geoffrey.

"Where is Katherine?"

"My dear wife is home with a stomach ailment."

"Not serious I hope?" Spencer didn't care for the worried look in Geoffrey's eyes.

"No. Not at all. She will be fine tomorrow I'm quite sure of it."

"No doubt," Spencer agreed and he hoped so. Although, she had been dealing with a difficult stomach lately. Could she be...? "How is married life treating you?" Damn, but he kept saying the wrong things tonight.

"As well as can be expected." Geoffrey set down his glass he'd just been handed on a small round table separating their two chairs. "I'm not complaining. Katherine is everything a man could ask for in a wife. I'm just finding the duties as earl pressing."

"They never have before?"

"No, they haven't." He looked across the room and frowned. "My brother seems in a rare mood."

William appeared to be winning at cards and drinking overly much. "Shall we drag him out of here while he can still stand?"

"Why not? It's time I got back to my wife."

CHAPTER THREE

MIRANDA FLUNG OPEN THE DOORS TO HER WARDROBE AND began tossing day dresses willy-nilly around her feet. "I can't find my favorite seafoam green day dress. The one with the yellow flowers embroidered around the hemline and down the sleeves," she said to her maid. She wanted that dress for afternoon callers because it highlighted her green eyes. Spencer had said he would call on her today, and she wanted to look her best. Oh dear, now she was even thinking like a love-sick fool.

"I'm sorry, milady, you dribbled jam on the bodice and I've not been able to get the stain out."

"Oh. Yes, I remember now." Her shoulders fell in disappointment. She surveyed the dresses around her feet, plucked up a buttercup yellow one with green ribbons and shook it out. "This one will do then. I'm sorry I made a terrible mess."

"Let's get you dressed and your hair styled so you can dazzle your gentlemen callers today."

Was she being that obvious? In recent memory, Miranda could not ever remember being so fussy about her clothing or hair. Yes, she always looked presentable, but now she wanted to look irresistible. Oh dear, what happened to her not wanting to fall in love or become betrothed until the end of the Season? She'd met a certain gentleman who stole the very breath from her lungs, that's what.

"You look lovely," Claudia said. "Who is this gentleman calling that has you worrying overmuch about appearance?"

"Is it that obvious?"

"I'm afraid, yes."

"A Mr. Stuart Spencer," Miranda said with a sigh. "He came yesterday as well. He is utterly handsome and witty. I finally met someone who doesn't mind my candid speech. In fact, I think he rather enjoys it.

"I'm happy for you, milady."

As Miranda made her way to the drawing room, she stopped several times and placed her hand on her belly. Butterfly wings caressed her insides, and she found herself lightheaded at the prospect of seeing Spencer again. If she didn't learn to control her feelings, she was liable to throw herself into his arms at the first possible opportunity. Causing a scandal and forcing him to offer for her was not what she wanted. True, she believed she wanted to marry Spencer, but she wanted him to want her. Not be forced into it.

Once she entered the warm, drawing room, thanks to the roaring fire in the hearth, she sat next to her mother on the burgundy settee.

"Unless we have an unexpected visitor, Mr. Spencer appears to be the only card which arrived this morning," Mother said with a frown. "I don't understand. You are beautiful and come from a prominent family. Why are there not dozens of prospective suitors banging down the door?"

"Perhaps because I don't possess a dowry?"

"Whatever gave you that idea?" her mother said in exasperation. "You have a more than generous dowry. I kept the money from your father. It is safe amongst my possessions."

"Then, why indeed?" Perhaps because the other suitors witnessed Spencer and her together and knew they didn't have a chance of a prayer in winning her affections. That must be it, otherwise, if Spencer did not offer for her, she had no one else willing to marry her. Her heart sank at the idea of Spencer not wanting her. But it also made her realize, if she could not marry him, she wouldn't marry at all. Her father would just have to find money elsewhere to save them from ruin.

Tears threatened to make an appearance as the butler entered the room and announced, "Mr. Stuart Spencer."

Instantly, her tears dried up and her pulse raced. Her mother must have noticed her change.

"Easy, dear," her mother whispered. "We don't want him to think you are *too* eager."

"Welcome, Mr. Spencer." Mother motioned with her hand to a chair facing them. The same one he sat in the previous day. "Please take a seat."

Mother leaned forward. "May I pour you tea?"

"Yes, please. One sugar, no cream."

"If my memory serves me, you had a wedding in the family recently," Mother said while she poured. "Will there be an announcement of an heir to come soon?"

The shock that flashed briefly on Spencer's face had Miranda troubled. He controlled his emotions quickly and plastered on a smile she knew he forced. She had witnessed him smiling often enough to know that wasn't genuine. *How odd.*

"My cousin, Lord Geoffrey, the earl wed. As of yet, there is no word of an heir."

"In due time I imagine."

Now he stared into his tea frowning. So Miranda changed the subject to the only one she could think of. "How is the weather today, Mr. Spencer?"

His eyes came up and met hers, his brows rose and he tilted his head almost as if he said thank you. The butterfly's fluttered again without hesitation.

"It is rather chilly I'm afraid. The clouds look ominous. It will probably be raining by the time I take my leave."

Before she could respond, her mother chimed in, "Spring can be such a disappointment. One day it's sunny and warm and the next day you need to sit by the hearth to ward off the chill."

"That is England for you." Spencer placed his china cup and saucer down on the tea tray and stood. "It has been my pleasure to join you both this afternoon, but I must beg my leave."

Once Spencer left the room her mother turned to her and frowned. "Well, he didn't stay very long. Have you done something to make him think you are not interested?"

Had she? No. Quite the contrary. Perhaps it was her mother asking family questions. Spencer obviously didn't relish speaking about them.

"No, Mother. I did not." She stood. "If you'll excuse me I feel a headache coming on."

Behind the closed door of her bedchamber, Miranda flopped down on her bed, turned onto her side, fluffed the pillows beneath her head and exhaled loudly. Spencer had acted strangely today. Had she done something to offend him? Her heart constricted at the thought. And as she closed her eyes to take a little nap and alleviate her headache, she'd not been lying about that, she envisioned her life without Spencer in it and she wanted to cry.

THE NEXT MONTH of the Season continued with one ball, soiree, and night at the theater or opera. Spencer and

Miranda danced, laughed and tried to steal away for intimate moments, but were always waylaid from someone in her family or his. The lack of privacy didn't hinder the love blossoming in her heart for him. However, something was different all of a sudden. She hadn't heard from him in two very long days. He'd missed afternoon tea, something he'd not done since they first met and Miranda's heart sank heavy inside her chest. What was keeping him from her?

That evening Miranda found herself attending a musical with both her parents at Lord and Lady Amesbury's. Their son's name had graced her marriage list but had already been crossed off due to his age and still attending university. That and she was in love with Spencer. As his name entered her mind she glanced across the room and saw him. Try as she might, she couldn't stop the smile that spread across her lips when his eyes found her. Nor could she ignore the quivering in her stomach and the urge to run across the room and fling herself into his arms. Too many gothic novels. They would be the end of her good reputation if she continued to devour them into the wee hours of the night. But she was so happy to see Spencer after he didn't call on her for two days. She'd sunk into despair of ever seeing him and his melting smile again. Not to mention, his handsome looks and good humor. She didn't think he'd lost interest in her. Not when he looked at her with such longing in his eyes.

That morning in the breakfast room, as she walked in, she caught the end of her parents' conversation. A conversation where Mr. Spencer's name was mentioned. Although, she didn't know if they spoke favorably about him or not. After a month of visits, she could only surmise that they were speaking in his favor.

During their afternoons together, her mother always seemed quite taken with him. Even hinting to her after he departed the very first time that he would make an excellent husband. And if Miranda let herself think about him as a husband, which she did often, her body tingled in places she never imagined could tingle. How embarrassing. Surely a proper lady didn't tingle down there? Except, every time she happened to be in his company she did...tingle...down there... that is. And sometimes moisture appeared. *Is there something wrong with me?*

"MAY I JOIN YOU?" Spencer bowed to both Lady Miranda's mother and father, then to her.

"Please do," her father replied. "How is your mother, Mr. Spencer? I've been neglectful in not inquiring before now. I kept thinking we would run into her at one event or another, but we haven't. Truthfully, we have not seen her since before your father's passing."

"She is well. Thank you for your concern."

"Did you know I attended Eton with your father?"

"No, I did not." Even though he and his father rarely agreed on anything, he still experienced a sudden pain in his heart every time his name was mentioned.

"Your father was quite the prankster."

Now that did shock him. "Really?" Hard to imagine his father, the stuffy, George Spencer, ever being young and attending Eton. Spencer remembered his days there well, and they were full of mayhem and mischief. Oh, he studied as well, his good grades attested to that, but what was the point of being young if you didn't enjoy yourself. Geoffrey, William, and he had some memorable moments within the hallowed halls of Eton.

"Oh, yes, he wasn't always the stogy gentleman he became after marrying your mother." Lord Chambers paused. "I apologize. I didn't mean any disrespect to your father's memory.

It's just he changed when he married and became a father, as we all do I suppose."

"No offense taken. He was a great father to me and my sisters even if he was a tad serious at times." At times was an understatement. Spencer often thought his father had never smiled a day in his life. What happened between his Eton days and the day he married his mother? No doubt his mother. She spent her days in bed with one pretend ailment after another. As long as he could remember, she'd been that way. It never bothered him, but he wondered if his younger sisters minded the fact that their mother didn't take an interest in their lives. Perhaps, but their grandmother made up for it immensely. There was nothing that went on in their family that she didn't know about or put her opinion on. And for that Spencer would forever love her. She represented his mother more than his mother did. Strange, how he'd forgotten his mother rarely left her room even before his father passed. For some reason he wanted to believe her behavior began after Father's death, not before. But the truth of the matter was, she'd always been that way as long as Spencer could remember. But why? Would he ever know the reasons?

Which reminded him, where was his grandmother this evening? She did love a good musical.

"Could I have your permission, Lord Chambers, to show Lady Miranda the lovely gardens all lit up at night with colorful paper lanterns?" William's voice intruded in his mind, *Are you bloody crazy? The gardens at night. Do you know how many ladies have been compromised and gentlemen forced to marry them by special license all because they took an innocent stroll in the gardens?* He promptly shut his cousin's voice down.

"You have my permission, but keep to the well-lit and well attended areas."

Mr. Spencer bowed. "You have my word, Lord Chambers."

When Miranda placed her hand on his forearm, heat scorched the spot and spread out until every inch of his body burned with desire. Nothing new, it had occurred each and every time they touched. He ignored the warnings his mind added to William's cautions and led Miranda out onto the terrace and into the well-lit gardens where colorful paper lanterns were strung together and hung everywhere he looked. To his disappointment, they were not the only young couple seeking privacy.

"Do you smell the jasmine?" Miranda inhaled. "It is my favorite scent. Not my favorite flower, that would be roses, but the smell of jasmine is intoxicating."

"Yes, it is rather distinct." What flower was she speaking about? All he could hear was his blood rushing inside his ears while he couldn't take his eyes off the creamy, white column of her neck where it met her collarbone. Then, of course, his eyes drifted down to the tops of her pale breasts straining against the confines of her cream colored dress. He'd never seen a lovelier pair of breasts begging to escape. His palms itched at the need to release them from their confinement.

Bounce them and test the weight of them in his hands.

Cup them to find out if they were a perfect fit.

Bloody bugger, get your mind out of scandalous thoughts. Too late, his cock strained against his breeches begging to be let out.

"Mr. Spencer. May I ask you a personal question?"

"Personal?" He didn't like the sound of that and his body tensed. Except then she laughed.

"Don't worry. It's nothing really, just about your cousin, Lord William, and why he doesn't appear to care for me?"

"Don't fret. Lately he doesn't like anyone." Not a nice thing to say about William, but the sad truth nonetheless. Ever since Geoffrey married Katherine, he had changed and not for the better. Gone was the affable cousin he knew. The way he'd lived his life carefree and happy until he found out his brother's secret. And when said brother married the love of William's life his unhappiness intensified. Poor William, forced to watch the woman he loved belong to Geoffrey. At least by law—the heart was another matter entirely.

"Oh, I'm sorry. Must be a rather lonely life if one keeps to himself and appears brisk so nobody dares approach him. Does he not want to marry someday? There are many debutantes this Season who would think it a privilege to marry the second son of an earl."

Did she want William for herself? Could he have misread her emotions and interest in him all this time? Was she being nice to him because she wanted to marry William? "Damn it."

"Excuse me."

"Begging your pardon. Are you interested in William?" His heart sank to his knees as he waited for her answer.

"Oh, no," she blurted out, then lowered her lashes. "No. I thought I made myself rather...that is...I thought you knew how I felt about you."

His insides switched from panic at thinking she wanted William, to elation. "I'm glad to hear this. As you deserve someone better than my cousin. Even if I think him a most honorable man. You want someone who will love and cherish you, not scowl on a daily basis beginning in the breakfast room." Funny, he never thought William took after his father until now. Had his father scowled all his life because he was in love with someone? And not his mother? If true, no wonder his mother spent her days in bed wallowing in self-pity. Assuming it was self-pity she wallowed in. He should be fortunate he had any siblings at all if that was the case between his parents. Enough about his family. This night was about Miranda and him.

Spencer turned down a path that looked quite deserted and not as well-lit as the rest. He shut out his promise to her father and William's warnings...again. Glancing this way and that and finding no one within sight, he pulled Miranda into his arms and waited for her to either pull away or sink into his embrace. He held his breath as he waited, and fortunately she didn't keep him waiting long. She sighed and relaxed against him, placing both her hands upon his chest and once again burning him to the core.

"Miranda?" He posed it as a question, but they both knew what was inevitable, unless she stopped him.

"Kiss me already. Spencer. The suspense is just about killing me."

Who was he to disappoint a lady? Cradling both her cheeks with his gloved hands, wishing they were touching skin to skin, he lowered his head and watched her eyes flutter closed as she leaned in further, trusting him.

When their lips met, Spencer's pulse soared at the first taste of her luscious, soft, pliant ones touching his. She seemed quite tentative at first then he let her curiosity take over as she moved her lips from side to side. Waiting patiently for his chance. And it came when she breathed in air, parting her lips, and he took advantage and the lead.

Although she startled when his tongue dipped into her mouth, she didn't hesitate before joining hers with his. This kiss, this mating of the tongues with Miranda, fueled his body as no other woman ever had before. What was it about her that set her apart from the numerous women he'd bedded over the years? Did he really care? No. What he cared about was her and making her first experience full of pleasure and making her want more, but only from him.

"Miranda." He paused to breathe, then took her mouth again, only this time in a punishing kiss, full of need, want, and desire. And she didn't shy away, she gave him as much of herself as he gave her. It was rough and primitive, but that was what she made him feel. He felt out of control and on the brink of sanity.

His mouth wanted to kiss her for eternity and more. His hands wanted—no—needed to travel up the inside of her skirts to find the warm heat between her thighs. Fingers, with a mind of their own, wanted to sink into her body and bring her pleasure.

Before he could stop them, his hands moved from her face to her waist. They skimmed up and down her sides. His thumbs caressed the outer edges of her breasts, and she moaned into his mouth, fueling his lust higher. This time, when his hands moved down, he caressed the front of her and cupped both her breasts in his hands.

Lost. He was lost. Well, almost lost. Not gone enough that he forgot where they were. Abruptly, he dropped his hands to his sides, detached his lips from her mouth and took a regrettable step back, hoping his legs didn't give way. They both stood staring at each other and gasping for air as time seemed to grind to a halt. The sounds of the nighttime bugs and voices and music from the distance faded into nothing until it was only two people who existed. He could spend all evening standing right in this very spot staring at her until the sun came up. Unfortunately, they could not.

Spencer exhaled with frustration because he did not want to break their connection, but he knew he must as they'd been gone far too long to be deemed proper.

"Miranda, please forgive me if I do not apologize for taking liberties. I've never wanted anyone as much as I want you." It was true and he didn't know what the bloody hell to do about it.

The elation in her eyes almost sucked him back in for another taste of her.

"I wanted the kiss, as much or even more than you did."

He skimmed his knuckle down her cheek and reveled as

her body trembled beneath his touch. "You shouldn't say such things to a man."

"You are not just *any* man, are you?"

Was he? No. He was the man who had fallen completely and irrevocably in love with her. "No. And I trust you will not let another man's lips touch yours."

"Never."

"Only mine." Had he just declared himself to her? Where was the panic? The tightening in his chest? The nausea settling in the pit of his stomach? None of it came. Perhaps when you find the one you are meant to love and spend the rest of your life with, it feels as natural as breathing. Being with Miranda was like breathing the cleanest country air possible.

"Do you think your father will give his approval?"

He need not say the rest. Miranda knew what he meant. Her eyes widened with excitement and her smile lit up her already gorgeous face, including the freckles he loved so much. He dropped a kiss on the tip of her nose.

"I will call upon him tomorrow."

ALL NIGHT long Miranda tossed and turned. She could not settle down. The knowledge that Spencer all but told her he loved her and that he was asking for her hand tomorrow kept her up with excitement. Her body hummed with awareness, and she relived her time in the gardens over and over again. Once, she almost slid her hand down between her legs then snatched it away at the last moment only to moan in frustration. She did cup her breasts, wondering what they had felt like to Spencer. Her nipples tightened, she dropped her hands down by her sides and exhaled.

The silly, lovesick smile she'd worn ever since the

encounter in the gardens would not leave her lips. If she had her way, she would smile for the rest of her life. And she would once she married Spencer.

Love.

She was in love with Spencer. Mr. Stuart Spencer. She would become Lady Miranda Spencer? Oh dear, she never asked if he minded if she kept her title when he did not possess one. She didn't believe he would mind. Would they marry in a senight with special license? Oh how she hoped so. She didn't want to spend another moment of a day without him. She would marry him tomorrow if it were possible.

Would her parents permit such a scandalous thing as not posting the banns? She sighed deeply. No. They would want a proper engagement and wedding for their only daughter.

That had her smile faulting and her heart skipping a beat. What if Spencer wasn't rich enough for her parents to even consider his offer? Truthfully, she didn't have any idea how rich he was. "Oh, please God, let him be rich enough for my parents to consent to this marriage." That was her last thought before she succumbed to a fretful sleep.

CHAPTER FOUR

THE FOLLOWING DAY DRAGGED ON. MIRANDA HAD HOPED Spencer would visit in the morning with her father and was frustrated beyond belief when he didn't.

"Mother," Miranda said as the proper hour for tea and visitations in the afternoon were concluding. "I was expecting Mr. Spencer. He said he was calling on Father today. Did he come and Father sent him away?" She buried her face in her hands and cried silently while her heart split in two. Ever since she'd woken up that morning, something had not seemed right. Her skin had itched with nerves and her stomach had been upset for no reason she could think of. And her heart had beat faster than usual and still hadn't resumed its normal pace. Her mind played tricks on her, she witnessed her future, and Spencer appeared nowhere to be found. Had her life ended before it even began?

"My dear." Her mother hugged her close. "I did not want to bring this up, but his cousin, Lord Geoffrey, was attacked and killed by highwaymen last evening and the family is in mourning. No doubt he will call upon your father when the time for mourning is over."

"H...how long will that be?" Her heart not only broke for the Spencer family, but for her.

"Hard to say. The widow will mourn for a year as will his brother and grandmother. As for the earl's cousins. It depends."

Miranda felt bad for thinking about herself and Spencer's marriage proposal when his heart must be breaking over the death of his cousin, whom he was so close too.

MIRANDA WAITED AND WAITED, as patiently as she could, for any word from Spencer. It came one morning when she least expected it and had resigned herself to never seeing him again.

My Dearest, Miranda,

As you well know, my cousin, Lord Geoffrey, is dead and William has inherited the title. I must beg your forgiveness for not writing to you sooner. Especially after how I left things during our last night together. Fear not, I will visit your father, in due time. The Spencer family has retired to the country and William has not taken the news of his brother's death well. He barricades himself in his study, refusing to allow anyone in, except his valet.

Grandmother is beside herself with worry and walks the halls of the estate at all hours of the night. My mother, per usual, traded her bed in London for a bed here. My younger sisters spend their days in the nursery, so nothing has changed for them and they are too young to truly understand.

Geoffrey's widow, Katherine, sits outside William's study door begging for entrance. How did our world become this? Needless to say, my family needs me. When I can assure myself all is well, I will travel back to London, post-haste, and approach your father. Until then, know I think of you.

Yours forever,

Spencer

She sat at her dressing table with parchment, quill, and ink and thought long and hard about the words she would put to paper. Spencer's letter brought her emotions close to the surface and she was afraid to express them to him. She did not want to convey her hurt for not hearing from him sooner. He did not need that guilt with all he had to deal with. After breathing in and out several times to relax she began.

Dear Mr. Spencer,

My condolences on the death of your cousin. So tragic and sad. I pray William, the new earl, and the late earl's widow, find comfort being surrounded by family. It says much about you personally, that you have stayed by their side during their time of grief.

I look forward to your visit.

Forever yours,

Miranda

FOUR MONTHS HAD GONE by since Spencer's cousin was killed. Although they had exchanged several more letters, her heart had almost given up on marrying him. She refused to acknowledge the anger seething inside her at being almost ignored by him. Surely he could take time away from his family and visit her and reassure her he still intended to propose.

The Season had long ended, and to her parents' dismay, no suitors sought out her affections. Miranda couldn't be happier. She had already decided, if she could not marry Spencer, she would become a spinster.

With a heavy heart, but hiding it well, Miranda attended Beatrice's wedding to Lord Frances Herman. The newly married couple were on holiday on the Continent, and she missed Beatrice most terribly.

Another fortnight ticked by, slow and steady, before Miranda and her family heard the newest tragedy to befall the Spencer family. Lord Geoffrey's widow was attacked and drowned in a stream on their country estate in Dover. Rumors had spread that it was the new Lord Bridgeton who committed the act. Lady Katherine was with child and it was surmised he couldn't risk an heir being born making him lose everything.

Such heartbreak to befall one family. Would the new tragedy keep Spencer from coming to her? Over the past several months she'd had doubts he truly loved her. This time a fortnight went by, then a month without word from him. Not so much as a hastily scrawled letter. When the appropriate year of mourning ended, she expected Spencer to arrive at her very door. A year from the day the earl died. He still didn't come. Her mother insisted she have another Season as they still needed money and a husband to provide for her. She flatly refused. Her heart died last year, and she didn't believe it would start up anytime in the foreseeable future.

Each day began like the last. She woke up with a heavy heart, dressed, had her hair styled, put on pretty slippers and joined her parents in the morning room for breakfast. More or less she moved her food around her plate as she had no appetite. And many times she asked herself why she even bothered to get out of bed. Melancholy had her in its grip, and she didn't know how to escape.

THE PAST YEAR, to Spencer's mind, was like living a nightmare that would never end. Every time he went to bed, he prayed the next day would bring relief. Unfortunately it never did. Would his heart ever be whole again and not pain him at every breath.

A senight after Katherine's death, their grandmother, accompanied by his mother and sisters traveled back to London, hopefully to quell the theory that William had murdered his own sister-in-law. As of yet, he had not been charged.

However, even Spencer could no longer take seeing the pain and anguish eat William alive. He'd become a shell of a man. He'd gone inside himself and wouldn't let anyone in. Even him. With a heavy heart, he left Dover for London six months to the day after Geoffrey was killed and went straight to Miranda's house. He prayed Miranda would forgive his absence and still cared for him as he did her.

To his surprise he was led directly to the viscount's study instead of the drawing room for tea. Indeed, he needed to speak with Miranda's father, but he rather hoped to feast his eyes on her first. The entire trip from Dover had his heart thundering and his stomach churning. Why he'd been so nervous, he could not say. He should have been excited to set eyes on Miranda again. But being led by the butler into the viscount's study had him quaking in his polished Hessians.

"Come in Mr. Spencer," said Viscount Chambers. "Please, take a seat and tell me what I can do for you today?"

After clearing the lump from his throat, he blurted out the words before the scowl Miranda's father gave him had him running out of the house. "I have come to ask for your daughter's hand in..."

"No."

Spencer could hardly believe what he heard and gagged as his lunch rose up his throat. "Did you say, no, Lord Chambers?"

"Yes and for several reasons. The first and most important

one being you broke my daughter's heart and she wants nothing to do with you. She said if you ever came calling to send you away. I'm sorry. But she has her heart set on someone else. Also, too much scandal is now attached to your family and I can't expose my daughter to it. She deserves the utmost respect from the *ton*. Being married to you will no longer provide her with that."

As Spencer left the Chambers' residence he hoped for a glimpse of Miranda to satisfy his heart for all time, but it wasn't to be.

Later that afternoon, not knowing how he'd gotten home to Bridgeton Manor, so numb was he, he found himself sitting in William's study. A study William no longer needed because he was in self-imposed exile in the country.

Yet he had to thank William, who was kind enough to leave a full decanter of whiskey on the desk. Brandy would not mend this broken heart of his. Nor would whiskey, but it would make him oblivious for a time.

CHAPTER FIVE

London 1818

"DUKE, DUCHESS. SPENCER BOWED TO THE HOSTS OF THIS evening's party in honor of Lord Sebastian Seabrook and Lady Teagan having recently wed. Spencer couldn't be happier for the couple. They seemed quite in love. Love? Yes...well...he'd been in love once many years ago, and then more recently with Isabella Seabrook, now married to the Earl of Northborough. The love he had for Bella wasn't quite what he'd encountered all those years ago with Miranda. He didn't know if age had anything to do with it. Twelve years was a long time since his first love. He'd been young and foolish. All he knew was, he wondered if he would ever again experience the vibrancy that came from loving Miranda?

He doubted it. Oh, he didn't begrudge his good friend Myles for marrying Bella. Any fool could see they belonged together. As did Bella's sister, Lady Amelia and his cousin, William. After twelve years of self-imposed exile, Spencer was thrilled William came to town following Amelia whom he'd met and fallen in love with in Dover.

Fortunately, fates were on their side as the true murderer of his brother and Katherine was exposed. Sir Phillip Trenton, Katherine's own brother committed the heinous crimes.

Spencer never believed all the gossip. He knew William was innocent, especially since Katherine and he were in love and it was his babe she carried when she died so tragically. So not only did William stay in the country for twelve years because people believed him a killer, he grieved deeply for his family and the love the two brothers shared with one woman. Two very different loves, but love nonetheless.

When Spencer had visited the Chambers' residence asking for Miranda's hand, he never imagined being turned away. She had refused him. The memory from that day was forever etched in his heart and mind. Something died inside him that day. Bella brought most of it back, but there were still pieces missing. He wondered if he would ever go back to the man he used to be before tragedy changed many lives, including his own?

It was a good thing William was married and would produce an heir soon. When they had a son, his grandmother would stop hassling him to marry and produce an heir in case something happened to William and he, God forbid, inherited the Earldom. He would do everything in his power not to let that happen. William would live to an old age with Amelia, their daughter, Olivia and many sons to come.

Surveying the crowd of usual members of the upper class had him helping himself to refreshments and seeking solitude in a corner. A corner with an empty chair.

"Is this seat taken?"

As soon as the words left his lips he was transported back in time. A time when he uttered the exact words to the same lady the second time he'd met her at Almack's of all places.

What the bloody hell was she doing in town? He hadn't seen her in twelve years. Why now? Why here? Not when he felt raw inside already this evening.

"I'm afraid it is."

Ignoring her, he sat anyway. *Taken*. She lied. He did a quick calculation in his mind as to her age now. Twenty-nine. The years had been kind to her, she looked much as she had at seventeen.

"I will vacate when the person who occupies this chair comes back to claim it," he said with a smug smile to himself. He may not have seen her in all these years, but he knew she'd never married, which made him wonder what happened to the man who replaced him in her heart. Her parents had both died long ago leaving her in the care of an aunt on her mother's side. Perhaps the aunt was attending this evening and insisted on Miranda escorting her.

"How have you been?"

The look she sent his way chilled his blood. Hatred shined out from her eyes. That couldn't be right? What had he ever done to warrant such distain? She'd sent him away, not the other way around.

"Why do you care, Mr. Spencer?"

Clearly, something was amiss. "I'm making polite conversation. But if you would rather I be silent, I will sit here and sip my wine, leaving you in peace."

"Thank you. That is most kind. Something that is not in your nature."

Not in his nature? What was she saying? "I believe I am and always have been and always will be, kind. I know not of what you speak."

The look again. Even with loathing shining from her intense green eyes, she looked more beautiful than he remembered. She was dressed splendidly in medium blue silk with cream accents. Her neckline may be a tad modest, but then it suited her age appropriately as most of The Beau Monde would consider her a spinster. Not he. She was anything but and his body stirred.

"Excuse me, I see my aunt sitting alone across the ballroom and I must attend her."

His eyes were riveted to Miranda as she walked gracefully, chin held high, across the room and stood to the side of a lady sitting with other equally elderly ladies. Poor Miranda. Did she spend her life with ancient people, doing ancient things when she should be living and loving?

"I know that look well, cousin," William said as he helped his expecting wife, Amelia, sit in the chair Miranda vacated.

"I don't know what you mean."

Laughter found his ears. The William of their days at Eton was back thanks to Amelia and her love and Sir Phillip for admitting to his crimes. Was there any hope he too could be the carefree man again? Bella brought it out in him, and most of it returned thanks to her, but not all. He'd kept a piece of his heart and soul locked away. Was Miranda the key?

"She looks much the same as I remember. Still beautiful," Spencer uttered the words before he could stop himself.

Amelia looked from her husband to him and back to her husband. "Who looks beautiful?"

"Lady Miranda Carlton," Spencer said with reverence.

"Who is she? I've never heard of her or met her?"

"She was the love of Spencer's life when tragedy befell our family. Her father refused Spencer's offer of marriage after Katherine's death. If I wasn't so lost in my own grief, I would have known about his own. I see it now."

"You do not," Spencer contradicted. "She is still beautiful, I give you that. But she was rude and hateful moments ago. Two things I can live without. Besides," he shrugged his shoulders and refused to acknowledge the pain that had seeped inside his chest at her cut, "I don't believe I will get the chance to make things right."

"Oh, Spencer, I'm truly sorry," Amelia said with a sigh. "Has she never married?"

"No."

She perked up in her seat. "Well, there is your answer. She is still in love with you."

"In love with me?" He stuttered. "Are you out of your bloody...?"

"Easy cousin," William chided. "That is my wife you're speaking to."

"Yes, well." Feeling chastised like a boy in the schoolroom, he sat back, crossed his arms on his chest, and seethed with righteous indignation.

"Where is she?" Amelia said as she turned her head this way and that. "I want to get a good look at her?"

Spencer ignored her as William pointed her out.

"Oh, she is lovely. I could speak to Bella, Emma, Amelia, Teagan and Penelope and we could help you by befriending..."

Spencer interjected. "Please don't. It would somehow come back to me and make things worse. She hates me for something I did. Even if I don't know what it is? I asked to marry her. I wanted to marry her. She refused me."

"Did you just admit to wishing you had married Lady Miranda twelve years ago?" Amelia said with a curious smile. "How utterly interesting."

"I'm glad I could amuse you this evening, Amelia, William." He rose, bowed, and went in search of the card room. And then he remembered Wentworth didn't believe in gambling and headed outside on the terrace instead.

When he saw who stood at the railing he almost made an about face but didn't.

"Lady Miranda, how exciting to see you again so soon."

She didn't bother to look at him. "Are you following me,

Mr. Spencer? Because if you are, please stop. I despise overly assertive men."

"I am merely getting a breath of the cool night air. And for your information, I do not need to be assertive with women. One look from me, and they usually invite me into their beds."

Her loud huff had him rethinking his cruel and shocking words. No doubt she was still an innocent at her advanced years.

"Funny, I don't recall inviting you into my bed all those years ago."

Lowering his voice and leaning close to her ear he whispered, "No. But I do recall a certain time in the dark gardens at the Amesbury residence and you sticking your tongue down my throat."

He should've seen the slap coming, but he didn't. When it did, he relished it. And he certainly deserved it. More than that, it made him feel alive again and gave him hope that if his insult moved her to violence, then perhaps she still harbored a tender spot for him after all these years.

"Forgive me, milady that was uncalled for. I bid you goodnight. Unless you would care for a repeat of what transpired between us twelve years ago. I hear the gardens here are lovely at night with the moon casting shadows all around."

With his heart hammering inside his chest, he bowed and backed away from her, wishing she would say something... anything to keep him standing right where he was. Or hope upon hope she would want a repeat of that incredible kiss that had haunted his dreams for years. Kissing her again would be like a taste of heaven...and hell. Always wanting more and never able to get enough. Doomed. His future was doomed.

❄

MIRANDA TURNED her back on Spencer so he wouldn't see her tears. Aunt Violet had insisted she enter into London Society during the Short Season and work her way up to the Season in the spring.

Personally, she would rather still be in Yorkshire taking her daily walks. But no, Aunt Violet was nearly out of money thanks to her no-good husband stealing everything she had two months ago. Two long and agonizing months. Her aunt had spent the last of her money on several new gowns for her. Against her will, she needed to marry. Just like the time when she was seventeen and had her first Season. What other choice did she have but to marry? Become a fallen woman and mistress to a wealthy gentleman? In her advanced years, nobody would want a mistress long in the tooth. Indeed, she would rather cut out her heart and feed it to wild dogs anyway. And she would be lucky to get any proposals of marriage. Her dowry no longer existed and rarely did a man marry without monetary gain. Which she possessed none of. Not to mention, she didn't know if she was capable of being a proper wife and all that entailed. The thought of performing her wifely duties and having a man's hands on her terrified her.

As she stood here weeping like a babe, she tried to come up with another way to procure the funds she and her aunt needed to live, other than marriage. Shame on her for inquiring about Mr. Spencer's marital status when they'd arrived in London. And begging her aunt to obtain an invitation to Lord Sebastian and Lady Teagan's engagement party. If word had come that Spencer had married, she would not be here tonight. Even after all these years, the pain of seeing him with someone else would have been unbearable. When word had reached her that he had, indeed, never married, her stomach had fluttered with elation. Much as it had when she'd spied him across the ballroom. It took all her self-control to look away and keep her eyes averted, knowing he was making a beeline straight for her. Somehow, she'd managed to keep her seat and not run toward him and make a fool of herself by flinging herself into his wonderful arms. Arms she'd ached to be held in over the years.

How embarrassing for thinking she could go through with the sham and flirt and woo Spencer to fall for her again. She could never do that because she realized something very important. When she witnessed him casually saunter her way, asking if the chair next to her was available, she found out she still loved him with everything she had inside her heart and soul. Even though he had never gone to her father and asked for her hand all those years ago, which broke her heart, she still loved him.

Oh, she tried for years to hate him but was never able to accomplish anything but anger and hurt. Eventually, those feelings changed back to caring and love. Why did he do it? Lead her on all those years ago only to decide not to propose? Waiting all those months while he mourned for his family members had paralyzed her. Fear, anger, hurt, need, desperation, and many more emotions plagued her on a daily basis. Never, in all her life, had she thought love not reciprocated would make a person die slowly inside until they existed in a lesser capacity.

Her parents could never understand her broken heart. They paraded every single, rich man in front of her for years to no avail. It was almost a blessing when they died of fever. Almost. She loved them and missed them every single moment of every day. She would give anything if they were here with her tonight. But the outcome would be the same. They needed money.

When she saw Spencer she had to bury her emotions deep down and act as if she didn't give a fig about him. A performance worthy of the Covent Garden stage if she did say so herself.

What confused her was the emotions she witnessed in *his* eyes. Surprise, excitement with a touch of lust. Just as she remembered his eyes doing all those years before. Except after those emotions, his eyes turned sad. Which she didn't quite understand. What did he have to be sad about? He was the one who never came for her. Left her with her heart ripped out of her chest and lying on the floor for any stranger to stomp on.

The entire time they talked just now her throat burned with unshed tears and her eyes stung. When she slapped him across the face and heard the gasps surrounding them, she almost begged his forgiveness. Never had she intended to hit him, but his words were so hurtful she just reacted to raw sensations churning inside her. Emotions making her crazy. Feelings and sentiments she didn't know if she could let them escape the locked box she'd put them in. She had wanted to come here tonight. She had hoped to see him. Then she did, and feelings exploded inside her, and she became confused and unable to cope so she lashed out.

Then she retreated to the terrace hoping to rein in her run-a-way thoughts and emotions, and who showed up? Him. Was he stupid not to see how torn up she was? For twelve years she nursed a broken heart. Oh, shame on her for letting her shattered soul rule her life. The truth was, she liked her life in the country. She'd always been a person who liked solitude. She had several proposals over the years, but she couldn't bring herself to marry a man who professed his love when she didn't, or couldn't, love him back. They deserved better. And she was nothing if not selfless.

Never once though, had she felt less of a woman without a man. Why were they taught early on in life that when they became of age, they would be introduced into Society and then marry and God willing, have children? To love, honor, and obey their husband.

Where were the words love, honor, and obey their wife?

Women were not objects to be desired, used for male pleasure then put aside until they needed the itch scratched again. Or wanted a pretty thing on their arm.

Perhaps she read too much and not always appropriate books. She particularly enjoyed reading this relatively new author, Mrs. Anne Smith. Such interesting and witty characters. And, of course, romance and love.

"Why me?" she mumbled.

"Excuse me?"

She pivoted around and came face to face with four complete strangers and the pregnant, Duchess of Wentworth with her lovely American accent.

"I'm sorry, Your Grace. I was woolgathering."

"Nothing to forgive. We all get lost in our thoughts at times. I saw you speaking to Spencer earlier and thought I would introduce my family to you. Bella, Countess of Northborough, Amelia, Countess of Bridgeton, Lady Teagan and Lady Penelope, this is Lady Miranda Carlton. The woman who stole our Spencer's heart many years ago according to Bridgeton."

"Bridgeton?" Miranda knew she'd heard the name before, but she couldn't place the title. It was as though a cloud smothered her memory.

"My husband, William Spencer, Lord Bridgeton. Spencer's cousin." The young countess with the lovely brunette hair and kind brown eyes said.

"Oh. Yes. I remember Will...I mean...Lord Bridgeton. Although he was not Bridgeton when I knew him." He married this young lady. Surely she must be half his age?

"It is a pleasure to make your acquaintance," Lady Northborough said. Spencer's most recent love interest, so she'd been told by her aunt.

"It is lovely to meet you," Lady Penelope said with a shy smile.

"It is a pleasure to make all of your acquaintances. And thank you, Duchess, for the invitation. My aunt and I haven't been in town for many years and as you might imagine, the invitations stopped arriving years ago. It was most kind of you to add us to your invite list at such short notice. My aunt is, or rather was, friends with the dowager and appreciated being given the opportunity to renew their friendship."

"She was thrilled to hear you were visiting London, and I imagine they are in a corner catching up on the years."

"I have no doubt."

"Please tell us something about Spencer from when he was young?" Bella asked with an inquisitive smile, making Miranda relax. She liked Bella and could not harbor any dislike for her for almost stealing Spencer's heart from her. Because truthfully, his heart didn't belong to her.

The memory of her first meeting had her smiling, recalling their conversation when dancing. A most wicked conversation to go with an equally scandalous dance. Although the waltz was not considered shocking anymore. "He was quite handsome and silver tongued."

"Oh, he is still both I can assure you," Bella said with a laugh.

"I'm glad to know that." Something inside her chest melted at hearing Spencer had not changed. "The first night we met we danced the waltz, which was considered most inappropriate at that time. When I think back, I can't believe my parents allowed it. But then again...never mind. We talked about unsuitable things. He made me laugh."

"Unsuitable?" Bella hinted with a smile. "Sounds like our Spencer. Care to elaborate on the conversation?"

Miranda's face heated. "I can't say. Well...maybe..." Heat warmed her cheeks at remembering the long ago conversation. "Actually, I can't."

The five women stared at her and smiled, warm genuine smiles, which had her smiling back.

"No need to. We all have had conversations with Spencer we wouldn't wish to repeat," the Duchess said.

Bella chimed in, "I had been waiting my whole life for Myles to propose. Spencer so graciously offered to help make him jealous. And I must say we had fun for a time."

"When my husband," Amelia added," arrived in London, after twelve long years, Spencer was shocked and enjoyed giving him a hard time in private. In public, he was like a mother hen daring anyone to speak or act disrespectful towards William."

"He really hasn't change at all, has he?" She couldn't stop her insides from melting.

"No." All the ladies spoke simultaneously.

Miranda remembered three young gentlemen who had graced her father's suitable husband list. Wentworth and Northborough, although they weren't Wentworth and Northborough then, as well as another friend of theirs she couldn't remember.

"I once danced with Wentworth, before he was the duke. Although I have to say, he was young and not in the least interested in me or any of the debutants as I recall," Miranda said thoughtfully. "I seem to remember he had quite a reputation. My parents had a list of gentlemen..." She hesitated, wondering how to explain.

"A marriage list," Bella said with a twinkle in her eyes.

"Yes, Wentworth and Northborough were on it. Although I don't know why, as I recall, they were still in university. Also, another gentleman they were friends with. I can't remember his name."

"Edward Worthington, now the Marquess of Amesbury," the Duchess supplied.

"Yes. It seems so very long ago." She paused and exhaled. "At other times it seems like only yesterday."

"Perhaps when we know each other better," Bella said, "you will share more of your first Season with us and stories of Spencer."

CHAPTER SIX

MYLES, WILLIAM, SEBASTIAN AND SPENCER STOOD INSIDE the French doors watching the ladies on the terrace.

"If I were you I would be concerned about what, Emma, Bella, and Amelia are saying to Miranda. I don't think you need to worry about Penelope or Teagan, as they haven't known you long enough," remarked William.

"Especially my wife," Myles said with a knowing grin.

"Yes, well, I believe my cause can only improve." Spencer raised his shoulders and lowered them.

"Your cause. Are you interested in Miranda...again?" William asked, shock on the edge of his voice

If it was up to him, he would walk away and never look back. But alas, his heart wouldn't let him. All the feelings he had for Miranda burst forth. Obviously, they'd only been buried beneath the surface. He couldn't walk away or give up until he tried to win her over again. He'd accomplished it once, how hard could it be twelve years later?

"It pains me to say that when I saw her tonight, my feelings from long ago resurfaced. My heart finally beat at full capacity after twelve years of not. And don't any of you laugh at me. You are all in love with your wives and know exactly what I mean."

"You do have me there, cousin. Would you like Myles and my help with this? We could tell her what an upstanding and honorable gentleman you are. That you dote on your elderly grandmother and two younger sisters. That you would make a perfect husband because you were raised with all women."

"I *was* raised with all women."

William looked at Myles and grinned. "My point exactly. Anyway, what have you got to lose? It's not as though any other women are knocking down your door."

"Nice, cousin, nice. Bloody hell, don't look now, but all six ladies are coming our way." He, however, couldn't take his eyes off Miranda and the graceful way she glided across the floor.

Myles stepped forward, bowed over Miranda's hand and Spencer wanted to take the man aside and pummel him to a bloody pulp.

"Lady Miranda, it is a pleasure to make your acquaintance. Call me Myles as all our friends and family do."

Bella put her hand on her husband's forearm. "Myles, Lord Northborough, may I present Lady Miranda. Please forgive his manners. He has always ignored *ton* standards and rules of etiquette."

"It is refreshing." She curtsied quickly. "A pleasure to meet you, Myles." Then she repeated her curtsy to Bridgeton. "It is nice to see you again, Lord Bridgeton."

Bridgeton bowed. "Likewise, Lady Miranda."

Spencer faded back and listened to the conversation surrounding him. For the life of him, he had no idea what anyone said. All he could do was stare at Miranda. The deep blue of her gown made her eyes appear more blue than green. The modest scooped neckline still managed to show off her breasts and he had to force himself not to stare at the creamy white swells. Several times, when he was not admiring her breasts, she locked eyes with him, nodded her head, blushed, and turned away.

Interesting. So she was not as indifferent to him as she let on. A waltz began playing and the married couples left to take the dance floor. Emma excused herself and left in search of her husband, no doubt. Penelope blushed profusely when a suitor came to claim his dance, which left Spencer and Miranda standing awkwardly. Since when did he tense up in the company of a beautiful woman? Since Miranda walked back into his life.

"Would you do me the honor of this dance?" He bowed at the waist and stayed down waiting for her reply. When it didn't come, he stood with his heart lodged in his throat.

Except when he looked at Miranda she smiled hesitantly and murmured, "Yes."

It had been twelve years since they danced together, but to Spencer it seemed like yesterday. She felt familiar and right in his arms. Natural as though they danced on a regular basis. And he had to admit, heavenly. Even through her dress and the layers of material beneath, her skin burned his hands. What he wouldn't do to get her alone in a dark room and touch her skin with his bare fingers. Gloves were a damn nuisance.

"Your friends are very nice."

"Yes, they are," he agreed.

"Your cousin's wife, Lady Amelia, is lovely."

Spencer noticed her frown. "What is it?"

"What do you mean?"

"You frowned when you said Amelia's name. Why?"

"Oh, nothing. It took me by surprise at how young she is. I was expecting someone more...my...age."

"They only recently wed. I don't know how much you know about him, but Bridgeton didn't leave his country estate in Dover for twelve years and only came to London during the last Season. Even I didn't see him for all that time. Wentworth was not favorable to the match at first. More like, he refused her to have anything to do with him. But eventually, he consented. Only an idiot would get in the way of love."

"Yes, only an idiot?

"I'm sorry."

"For what?" she asked shyly.

"For whatever I did to make you hate me."

"I don't hate you, whatever gave you that idea?" Her cheeks turned a becoming shade of pink.

Hope. Her words and her blush gave him hope. "May I call on you tomorrow? Perhaps we could go for a ride in the park?"

"I would like that very much."

When the band finished the last cord, he escorted Miranda to an empty chair and strolled away elated with hope. And a stupid grin plastered on his face for all to see. More than one person looked at him rather strangely. Bloody hell, he didn't care if he looked like a love-sick fool, his insides were bursting alive.

This night was like living the night they first met all over again. This time the outcome of their relationship would be different. At least he hoped so. He didn't think he would survive her refusal of marriage a second time. Did he really plan on proposing to Miranda?

"Auntie, Mr. Spencer will be calling on me soon to take me for a ride in the park. At my age, I do not think I need a chaperone. Besides, if I am to find a rich husband soon, I must have time alone with him to...ah..."

"To seduce him, my dear," Aunt Violet said with a twinkle

in her eye as they shared tea in the drawing room of the modest townhouse they had rented in London, just on the outer fringes of Mayfair.

"Don't look shocked. I've been married three times and widowed twice. Seduction is nothing new to me. In fact, if I could find a gentleman my age looking for a companion, I'd be more than willing to comply. Nights are cold, lonely and long. I am not so very old you know."

"Auntie." Miranda laughed. She was used to her aunt's frank speaking. Perhaps that's where she got that most annoying trait from. Speaking her mind had only gotten worse the older she became. That and people were more relaxed in the countryside. She would do well to remember she was in London now, where social etiquette meant everything.

"I do not plan to seduce Mr. Spencer." She frowned, not at all confident she could put aside her fears and seduce anyone. "More likely he will try to seduce me if my memory serves correctly." Her skin tingled at the idea of Spencer seducing her. Quick as the thought and feelings burst upon her, they left, leaving her chilled and weary. Could she even allow herself to be seduced? Touched intimately after what happened to her? Only time would tell, she supposed.

"Would that be so terribly bad, dear, if he seduced you? God did not intend women to be without men."

"Auntie?" She shook her head.

"Well, he didn't. Take Adam and Eve."

"Enough." She held up her hand. "I understand. But really, Spencer is different. He would see right through my deception. The thing for me to do is be honest, up front. Tell him I need to marry him for his money. Without him and his money, you and I will have to live in the rookeries of St. Giles."

"Hardly, my dear. We would never survive there. Please

take my advice and seduce him first. Honesty later. It worked for me three times. Good outcomes twice, although they died. The third, well, we know what happened with him. He'll find himself in hell eventually for what he did to you. Meanwhile, you must think of yourself. I know it sounds self-ish, and you are nothing but selfless. It goes against all your beliefs to use Mr. Spencer like you must. But in the end, I believe all will be forgiven. I saw the way he looked at you last evening. Any attendees, who bothered to look at him, really study him, would've seen a man with love shining in his eyes." Aunt Violet paused and took a sip of tea, then continued. "You are actually doing him a favor by marrying him and giving him heirs."

"I mean no disrespect, Auntie, but how is tricking him into marrying me doing him a favor?"

"Enough of this nonsense. Go make yourself presentable because your young man will be here soon, and you need to be at your most beautiful."

Didn't her aunt always tell her she was beautiful? Why then did she need to be more beautiful? Very well, she would try her best to sweep Spencer off his feet and get him to mutter three little words. "Will you marry me?" Her mistake, four words. Miranda dressed in a deep green riding outfit that brought out the color of her eyes and complimented her hair which was more blonde than strawberry-blonde these days. Something she didn't mind at all. She donned a matching bonnet, pelisse and puff to ward off the late day chill. Black, half-kid boots graced her small feet. She paced back and forth in the drawing room, wringing her hands together until they cramped. Would Spencer think it odd she would receive him alone. And where was her aunt? She could use her support right about now.

"A Mr. Stuart Spencer," announced the butler and she turned and all breath vacated her lungs at the sight of him in splendid buff breeches, brown claw-hammer coat, and matching hat. Along with his cream colored shirt and cravat, polished brown Hessian's completed his outfit. She couldn't ever remember witnessing a finer looking gentleman.

"My dear. Lady Miranda," he said as he strolled toward her, never taking his eyes off hers. Eyes intense and intruding. He turned out a perfectly elegant bow. "Shall we go riding?"

She placed her hand into his gloved one and let him escort her out the door, down the stairs, and to the side of his high perch phaeton.

"I hope you don't mind riding in the open. It is a rare sunny day and nothing feels better than warm sunshine while riding."

At her first look at the coach she cringed. It was high off the ground, and she'd heard all sorts of things about how unsafe this new mode of carriage was. Regardless of the warnings, she also heard it was all the rage. Spencer helped her up the stairs. Once she was settled he removed them, joined her, and took the reins to the matching set.

They entered through the gates of Hyde Park and joined the other carriages and people on horseback parading to be seen on Rotten Row.

"Slow going today. I think the whole of Society had the same idea. Not that I'm complaining. I get to be with the most beautiful lady in all of London Town." He took his eyes off the path and leisurely looked her up and down with an intensity that caused her cheeks to burn.

"Flattery will get you nowhere, Mr. Spencer." She tried to heed her aunt's words about seducing first, honesty later, but that wasn't who she was. Dishonesty wasn't in her nature, at least not when it came to Spencer. She only hoped she didn't live to regret ignoring her aunt's advice. To calm her nerves and give her courage to ask what she must, she inhaled, exhaled and focused on the carriage and its occupants in front of them. "May I ask you a serious question?" She had to explain her situation now before she lost her nerve.

"By all means."

"I find myself in a rather delicate situation. My aunt's latest husband ran away to America and took all the money and sold the house out from under her. We are broke. Will be tossed out on the streets at month's end." This was harder than she thought. She felt like a beggar in the streets with her hand out looking for a shilling or whatever she could get.

"Go on, now that you have piqued my interest." Damn him, but he did look most interested.

She looked away for courage. Because if she looked at him she would falter and not utter another word about her situation. "Fine. I will just say it. I need a husband. A rich husband." After the words came out she gulped for air, not realizing she'd been forgetting to breathe.

"Yes."

"Yes? Yes to what?" Her gaze moved to Spencer who looked straight ahead, although he appeared to be smiling. The man was insufferable. He was enjoying himself at her expense.

"I will marry you. Isn't that what this conversation is about? You are asking me to marry you so you and your aunt will have some place to live...and money?"

"Well," she sighed, "put that way it sounds rather like we are using you."

"Are you not?"

"Actually, it goes both ways. I use you for your money and you get your heirs." Fear curled around her heart at the thought of giving him heirs. Perhaps he didn't want a real marriage, and she would not be subjected to perform her wifely duties.

He became very still and quiet, making her even more nervous.

"Heirs?" He choked out sounding rather shocked.

Oh my, was the thought of making heirs with her appalling to him? Sheer force of will had her speaking. "You do want an heir, do you not?"

"I had resigned myself to never marrying and having one. I had come to terms with it. But if you're willing to give me heirs, who am I to refuse such a generous offer. Although," he paused, "and please forgive my ignorance and bluntness, but aren't you a bit old for producing heirs?"

His hurtful words struck her mute and had tears pooling in her eyes until she looked at his amused face. Was he making fun of her? Fun of her dire situation? Before she could say anything, he turned off the heavily traveled path, down a deserted one, and pulled the coach off to the side. He turned in his seat, looking grim. Perhaps he hadn't been making fun of her. Perhaps in the beginning he had, towards the end he became strangely subdued.

"Miranda." He transferred the reins to one hand and gently placed his hand on her cheek, his eyes soft. "When I first saw you the other night, I couldn't for the life of me understand what brought you to London after so many years. Now it makes perfect sense. Also, why you chose Wentworth's. You did your homework and you knew I would be in attendance. Since when did you become such a calculating person? I don't know if I should be proud of you or horrified. But I do know this." He glanced right and left then leaned toward her. "You will propose marriage to no other. I will marry you this Saturday. I will send word to the Archbishop of Canterbury and procure the special license we need."

Once again, she forgot to breathe as his lips lightly caressed hers. When he pulled back and grinned wide, she wanted to curl her fingers into his lapels and drag him back for a real kiss. A kiss like the one he gave her when she was seventeen and naïve to the world. Before her tender, young heart had been broken.

Before she knew what he was about, he had the carriage moving and they were at her rented accommodations minutes later. He escorted her to the door and bowed. "I will send word as to the arrangements."

He left her standing on the landing as the butler opened the door. What did he expect her to do? Wait to hear from him. Sit and drive herself mad with wondering what he was thinking? What he was planning? She had waited once before and it hadn't turned out so well.

She stomped, most unladylike, into the house and entered the drawing room where she found Aunt Violet having tea. After sinking into a chair she muttered, "Such an infuriating man."

"He turned you down?" Auntie said with a frown.

"No. He accepted." When he arrived to take her to Hyde Park she had planned to do as her aunt suggested and flirt and bat her lashes at Spencer. Who, no doubt, would have been suspicious right away. Because, never had she ever, batted her lashes before. It was downright silly in her opinion. A gentleman either favored you or he didn't. Making a fool of oneself would not change his mind. Anyhow, when she left with him she didn't expect to return betrothed. Even if she had been the one to ask. Actually, she never did ask. She had implied she needed to marry and he, if her memory served her said, "I will marry you." How had that happened? Had he somehow known before today that she needed to marry and planned on making it happen? How could he? The only ones who knew were her aunt and herself. And now she could not ask him because he said he would send word with the arrangements. Not only was he infuriating, he was insufferable as well. And overconfident and...so many more things she could hardly think of them without wanting to scream.

"Relax, I'll pour you some tea, it never fails to help settle one's nerves." Her aunt's frown transformed into a wide smile.

"He said he would send word when all the arrangements are made. Obviously, he thinks I will wait and wait just like last time when he never came." Closing her eyes she fought the tears which insisted on making an appearance. After all these years one would think she had gotten over her heart being broken. Obviously not. And she'd known that the moment she had set eyes on him at the Wentworth's ball.

"My dear," her aunt began. "History will not repeat itself. He would not have said he would marry you if he didn't mean it."

"How do you know," she asked around a hiccup.

"Just a feeling. Now I think the lovely ice blue gown will make a beautiful wedding dress."

"It's what I had in mind when I picked it out. But what am I supposed to do on my wedding night?"

"Whatever your new husband wants."

"Whatever he wants? What if I can't bring myself to..." her cheeks warmed and she touched them with the tips of her fingers. "What if I can't? What if the next morning he decides he made a mistake and has the marriage annulled? I'll never be able to show my face in London again. More importantly, we will have no money and no place to live. Oh my God," she cried. "This is too much. No, no, no, I can do it. I must do this."

"My dear, I have all the faith in the world all will be well. Trust me on this?"

Trust her? Could she?

CHAPTER SEVEN

"I'M GETTING MARRIED ON SATURDAY," SPENCER SAID AS HE walked into the drawing room of his townhouse to find his mother, grandmother, and two sisters, Elizabeth and Mary, all staring with their mouths open over their tea cups.

"Yes. You heard me correctly. I have asked Miranda to be my wife, and we want to be married immediately. The only problem is where to hold the service."

"St. James Duke's Place is well known for marriages and is such a lovely church. Have the service there and the wedding breakfast here," his grandmother said with an elated smile. "I must say it is about time you grew up and married and put down roots."

Spencer couldn't come up with a suitable thing to say to his family. He bid them farewell, walked the half-a-mile to his cousin's townhouse where he found William and Amelia hosting Bella and Myles for tea.

"I have news," he said breathlessly from his hasty walk. "Miranda and I are getting married this Saturday."

As with his family, four sets of eyes looked incredulously at him.

"Congratulations." Bella stood and gave him a hug. "I am so very happy for you. I like her. She has personality and you will not get bored with her."

"Congratulations," Amelia said. "This is great news, is it not William?"

"Yes. It is the very best."

"If you ladies will excuse us gentlemen, I would like a word in private with William and Myles."

Once the three men were behind closed doors in William's study, each holding a glass of brandy, Spencer spilled his guts.

"She asked me to marry her because she and her aunt are broke. Well, truthfully, she never asked. She stated that she needed to marry someone wealthy, and I told her I would marry her. Spencer broke out laughing. "I can't believe my luck? I'm finally going to marry the woman I should've married twelve years ago."

"No wonder she came to town. She planned this. Why the conniving little..."

"Easy cousin that is my betrothed you are insulting. I don't care if she is using me or not. In time, she will come to love me again. I know it. And if she doesn't...well...it won't be the first marriage to go loveless."

"What is your opinion, Myles?" Spencer asked, wanting an opinion besides his biased cousin's.

"Me." Myles downed his glass, and Spencer knew he was trying not to laugh. "I think you are a lucky man. Lady Miranda is beautiful. A little long in the tooth, but not that long."

"Exactly what I think. Twenty-nine is still young enough to bare children. Why my mother had Mary when she was thirty-two. Clear your calendars for Saturday as you all have a wedding to attend."

THE MORNING of her wedding found Miranda's entire being vibrating with nerves. And if she was truthful with herself, not just with anxiety, but excitement as well. She would finally marry the man she fell in love with at seventeen. The man who shattered her heart and dreams and propelled her to live as a spinster.

All was forgiven. Her shattered heart and dreams were whole. All that mattered from this day forth was the future. The past would stay in the past. She'd spent years loathing Spencer and loathing herself. No longer.

Her chance at happiness was within reach. Spencer was within her grasp. In one-hour she would be married...to *him*.

Her hand flew to her stomach as an extended family of butterflies took flight.

"Oh my dear," Aunt Violet exclaimed as she entered her chamber. "You look positively divine. Claudia outdid herself with your coiffure. And the dress shows off your figure perfectly. Clingy in all the right places. Spencer will be struck mute when he sees you walking down the aisle."

"Thank you." She spun around and looked once more in the mirror, her reflection making her feel like a fairy princess on her way to marry her prince.

She descended the stairs on her aunt's arm, entered the carriage Spencer provided for them, and arrived at the small, intimate church. Bridgeton, looking dashing in formal wear greeted them. "May I escort both you lovely ladies down the aisle? Spencer thought you would enjoy the escort."

"Thank you." And she was thankful as she had wondered when they pulled up to the church how she would ever manage walking in her bundle of nerves state. So now, Miranda found herself between Bridgeton and Aunt Violet and walking, oh-so-slowly down the aisle toward Spencer who took her breath away, made her knees wobble and her hands vibrate with the urge to hold him close to her heart.

He looked handsome dressed completely in white. The contrast between his dark hair and light clothing was startling. Never had she seen a gentleman look as handsome as he. Since her eyes were riveted on her husband-to-be the entire time, she was shocked when she reached his side and they faced the vicar together.

As the vicar spoke and she recited her marriage vows in a soft voice, she gleamed at Spencer. It was foolish of her to let him see the love she had for him shining in her eyes, but it couldn't be helped. Over the course of her entire life, she had struggled to keep her emotions from showing. This, being the happiest day of her life, was not the time to squash her feelings. She did not know if Spencer still loved her, but she would persevere regardless. She would love him enough for both of them.

When they were pronounced man and wife, her eyes widened at the lovely emerald and diamond ring gracing her left-hand ring finger, and then her knees almost gave way at what it implied. Finally, she married the love of her life and would experience the marriage bed. She would not acknowledge the little bit of unease suddenly spreading through her body.

The wedding breakfast seemed to go at a snail's pace. The dining room, where it was held, was huge and the servants hustled about. She, nor any of their guests, wanted for anything. It was a pleasure to finally be meet Spencer's sisters. Mary was the epitome of a young, blonde, blue eyed debutante—quiet and painfully shy. Elizabeth's blue eyes sparkled with mischief, much as Spencer's did on occasion and possessed his dark hair. Way back when, Spencer's sparked with mischief always. Now, he held his emotions back, only on occasion, giving her a glimpse into the Spencer of old. Today she prayed things would change. That he would become the carefree man she first fell in love with. Because she wanted nothing to be between them. She'd told him the truth of why she needed to marry, now she could work to proving to him it was love that brought her back. Love more than money. And she hoped that love would sustain them for the rest of their lives.

She remembered meeting Spencer's grandmother many years ago, but not his mother. Spencer explained that she always suffered from one ailment or another. Although never anything serious. Thankfully, she felt healthy enough to attend today, although she paid little attention to anyone. Grandmother, on the other hand, beamed with pride and happiness.

So now she sat at this enormous table with Spencer's closest friends and family. Oddly enough, she felt strangely at ease. Although a bit nervous at the thought of sharing the house with so many members of his family. Hopefully their rooms were far apart giving them some privacy. Aunt Violet would also be staying with them for a spell. Miranda wanted her nearby if she needed someone to talk to about the past.

Finally, all their guests departed, after eating, drinking, and wishing them well. The remainder of Spencer's family and her aunt made themselves scarce, no doubt retiring to their rooms after such a long and exciting day. So now she found herself being escorted to the wing of the house that occupied their rooms, and she was elated they would finally get their privacy. At least she believed so.

"Your home is lovely. I believe I can be comfortable here. Your family was most kind and gracious to me considering how shocked they must be at our sudden nuptials."

"Yes, well." He cleared his throat as he opened a large wooden door leading to beautiful rooms. "They were shocked. But do not fret. I didn't tell them the truth in the matter. And they don't need to know about it. I have purchased the home you and your aunt were renting for her and set her up with an allowance. No one needs to know of your dire situation or the reason for our marriage. It is between the three of us. Although, I may have told Myles and William, but they don't count. They would never break my confidence without my permission."

"You told..." She honestly felt a little sick at what they must be thinking of her.

"I know that look, but please, they don't think badly of you."

"Badly of..."

"Forgive me. My words are not coming out as intended." He gestured to the room with his hand. "How do you like your accommodations? These rooms once belonged to my father and mother. No one has inhabited them since my father's death. Everything has been cleaned and prepared for our use. There is a dressing room and behind the screen a tub and wash basin. My rooms are through this door."

He opened the door connecting the rooms and turned toward her. "If there is anything else you need, please do not hesitate to ask Mrs. Noble, the housekeeper. She has been with us forever. If it pleases you, I will send your maid right up."

"Yes, thank you."

Spencer bowed, took her hand in his and brought it to his lips. His lips brushed against the inside of her wrist between the glove and her dress sleeve causing her to shiver and goose bumps to cover her skin.

"I have several things to oversee. I will come back when I'm finished."

Shocked. She was *shocked*. He left her on their wedding day to oversee things. What things could be more important than them? What an exasperating man. And she married him? She had to be out of her mind to think that once they were married they would live happily-ever-after like the fairy tales her mother used to read to her as a young child.

She huffed and sat down on the edge of the four poster bed, acknowledging the beauty of the room. Cream and light green made for a soothing and romantic atmosphere. Obviously, her new husband didn't think so. How could he not look at the inviting bed, with dozens of pillows and the thick coverlet, and not want to take her to bed. "It's my wedding day," she whispered out loud. "Does he not desire me?"

What man leaves his bride moments after the wedding celebration ends to take care of things? *Hers*. Perhaps she just made the most horrible mistake ever in marrying someone she thought she knew? Had he changed so very much that he had no feelings for her whatsoever? Didn't care that she sat here, pain radiating from her heart, making it hard to breathe?

A soft knock on the door turned out to be a good distraction as Claudia entered, followed by several footman carrying her trunks. She and her maid spent the better part of an hour unpacking all her belongings.

"If there is nothing else you need from me, I will go and see to your bath. Mr. Spencer informed the cook that the two of you would be dining in your rooms." She curtsied and left.

How did she feel about dining in private? Uncertain. At least if they dined with his family and her aunt there would be conversation going on around the table. Here, alone with Spencer, the only conversation would come from either of them.

She so fervently wished the years would roll back to when they were comfortable with each other. Most definitely

Spencer had made her nervous then, but she never felt at a loss for words or what to say in his company. Now, no matter what she intended to say, something else came out entirely. Usually something rude or mean.

Could she manage to hold her tongue to sugar and sweetness during dinner? She would even if it killed her. Spencer was kind enough to marry her, the least she could do was act civil in his company. Obviously, it was time for her to lock back up her love for him and treat him with polite disregard as he'd done to her.

Civil...polite...disregard? Oh, how she wished for more. So much more. Love. What a fool she was to want love. She wanted to see him look at her like the duke looked at his duchess. As Bridgeton looked at Amelia and Northborough at Bella. Was that too much to ask?

Perhaps. Perhaps not. Only time would tell.

Not long after her maid exited did several under-footmen come carrying buckets of hot water for her bath. And when she sank into the steaming hot, jasmine scented water, she sighed with relief. He remembered her favorite scent, that had to mean something, did it not? Or was it pure coincidence?

After bathing, Claudia helped her dress in a lovely, cream linen night rail and dressing gown trimmed with gold ribbon that must be courtesy of her husband as she didn't own such fine bed clothes. He expected her to dine in her night clothes? Perhaps that was what married people did when they dined in their private chambers.

She waited patiently on the chaise in front of the blazing hearth. The warmth coming off the logs had her heart slowing, her eyes drifting closed, and she sank into a light sleep only to be awoken by a caress from a large, warm hand trailing down her cheek.

"Wake up, my dear. Our dinner has arrived."

"Oh." She blinked and found her eyes taking in her husband dressed in a navy dressing robe. "I didn't mean to fall asleep. Have you been here long?"

He smiled and held out his hand to offer his assistance in helping her rise. "Only for a moment. Although, I have to admit, I felt guilty waking you. You appeared so peaceful in sleep. And so very beautiful."

Hearing him call her beautiful had her heart singing with hope.

He seated her at a small table the servants must have brought in with the food while she slept more soundly than she believed. When she inhaled the delicious scents, she nearly drooled, causing her stomach to growl. It was then she realized she'd not eaten a thing since their wedding breakfast celebration and was famished.

"May I serve you?" he queried.

"Please."

Miranda watched as Spencer put a small sample from each dish on her plate along with a piece of bread spread with cream. Not knowing where to begin, as everything looked delicious, she stabbed her fork into a small white roasted potato and asparagus coated with cream. "I can't believe cook outdid herself after this morning's fare, but she did."

"I agree." He held up a crystal decanter of red wine. "Would you care for some?"

"Please."

All this formality was beginning to cause a strain in her spine. Sitting so rigidly went against her body's natural posture, and she willed herself to relax.

Once he filled his plate, he sat down and began eating in silence. Every now and then he would glance at her. But other than that he spoke not a word. Didn't he know how difficult this was for her? Not knowing whether he had pretended he wanted to marry her. Was he here because he wanted to be or because he was doing her a favor?

Why had she not thought this through? Never had she imagined this awkwardness between them.

The servants came and cleared the table and chairs and she sat on the chaise while Spencer took a seat on a cream covered chair.

"That was delicious. I'm full to near bursting."

"It was good," Miranda agreed.

"When you feel up to the task, you can take over for my grandmother in overseeing the menus and other household duties the lady of the house takes care of. I haven't a clue what that entails."

"Thank you. Will your grandmother mind?"

"She will be thrilled. Perhaps she and my mother will retire to the country. Although I don't see that happening until Liz and Mary are wed. Meanwhile, more importantly, will you be comfortable with so many family members around?"

"Yes. Of course. Why wouldn't I be?"

His eyes widened. "Because of our arrangement?"

"Arrangement?"

"Yes. How long do you think we can convince them we are a normal married couple before they realize we sleep in separate beds?"

"Oh," was all she could manage to say. Her throat clogged from the lump forming there. Did he mean not to sleep with her? Not take his husbandly rights?

"But I told you I would give you an heir."

"Yes. I remember word for word what you said. But understand this." He narrowed his gaze on her, making her squirm. "I will not bed you until you ask me. I will not make you be obligated to me. Besides, perhaps I've changed my mind about children. They can be a nuisance, you know."

He stood, stretched, and turned toward her. "Goodnight my dear. I hope you sleep well."

After he left, her heart sank heavy inside her chest as she climbed beneath the coverlet and dwelled on what a mess her life had become. Had she misread him completely? Had she let her dreams of a fairy-tale wedding and marriage cloud her to his real idea of what their marriage would be? It took nearly an hour for her mind to settle down enough to drift into restless sleep.

AFTER THEY DINED, it took every ounce of restraint Spencer possessed to walk away from Miranda. When he'd first entered her chamber and found her asleep on her chaise, his heart expanded inside his chest. And that wasn't the only thing that grew in size.

He'd wanted to join her and make sweet love to her right there with the fire roaring in the fireplace. Strip her down so he could finally see what she looked like naked instead of relying on his imagination and dreams.

But that wouldn't be fair to her. She needed to eat. Was probably as famished as he was. Many hours had passed since the wedding breakfast. Which brought his mind back to when he first glimpsed her walking down the aisle toward him on William and Aunt Violet's arms. His heart had pounded like a drum inside his chest, causing his blood to pump through his ears so fast he'd gone deaf. The light blue dress she wore flowed down her body, accentuating all her womanly attributes, causing his mouth to go dry knowing she was finally his for the taking. Except was she? He wanted her to be completely and irrevocably in love with him before he bedded her. He craved her love. He didn't think he would survive without it. So he did the most gentlemanly thing he could do—left her untouched on their wedding night. He would wait until she loved him in return before he would bare his soul to her. It was the only way he could protect himself from her. Because if he made love to her tonight, he would be unable to hold back his feelings for her and he was afraid. There. He let his mind think it. He, Stuart Spencer, was afraid of Miranda Carlton. Petrified of the intensity of his feelings for her.

When he skimmed the palm of his hand down her soft cheek while she dosed, he'd swallowed a groan. Oh, many times over the years, he'd dreamed of being with her like this. Only to awaken sweaty and tangled in his sheets and so very alone.

He still had a difficult time comprehending his good fortune. Thank God he hadn't listened to his grandmother and mother and settled by marrying someone else. His body shivered at the horror.

He would forever be grateful for another chance with her. And this time he would not muddle it up. Not that he did before. Someday soon they would have to address the past. But not tonight.

Dinner had been a quiet affair. He was uncomfortably aware of her nerves. Did she think he would tear her clothes off and fall onto her the moment the food vanished?

How he wished he had inside knowledge of what was going on in her pretty head. He wanted to ease her mind that he wasn't a barbarian and he would give her time to adjust to being married to him. Taking a woman without her wanting him, no matter what the law said he could do, was not in his nature.

The first time they came together as husband and wife Spencer demanded they both desire it more than anything. It went without saying that he wanted it more than life itself. In

Miranda's case, he didn't believe so. At least not yet. But he would woo her until she did.

She was, after all, a twenty-nine-year-old innocent. His insides churned and he frowned. At least he thought she was innocent. And if she wasn't? It didn't matter. Innocent was not something he'd been since the tender age of fifteen. But of course, society dictated that men could have sexual relations before marriage. Not the same for women. At this moment in time, all that mattered to him was getting Miranda to fall in love with him so he could show her how much he loved her in return.

How he'd never stopped.

How a day never went by without his mind drifting to her.

How his body had ached for her year after year after year to no avail.

When he'd met Bella, he'd allowed himself to dream of a life with her. Even had convinced himself he was in love with her. Loved her—yes. In love—no. It took twelve years of maturity to realize he would be in love with no other but Miranda. So he had resigned himself into knowing, if and when he married, love would be vacant.

Little did he know Miranda would step—no—crash into his life and offer herself up on the altar of marriage.

When he'd left her this evening, on her chaise, looking like an angel and a courtesan at the same time, it killed him.

Would she have allowed him to make love to her? The point was moot. She would have to make the first move. He refused to take advantage of her. But how the bloody hell did he manage to live under the same roof as the woman of his dreams and not show her how much he desired and loved her?

Sheer force of will. She must make the first move. She needed to want him. He would not take advantage of the trust she had in him.

Trust he didn't take lightly.

Sleep eluded him that evening as he tossed and turned wondering what Miranda was doing. Was she sleeping? Dreaming of him? Congratulating herself on not having to have marital relations with him?

Finally, as the sun snuck through the crack in the drapes, he drifted off from complete exhaustion.

CHAPTER EIGHT

AFTER TAKING BREAKFAST IN THE MORNING ROOM AND finding it void of any other members of his family including his wife, Spencer entered his study and wondered what to do to occupy his time today. To make the day go by faster because he had the feeling it would linger suspended in air. Yesterday he had done any paperwork necessary which left him with nothing on his agenda for today.

He could visit his club? Or his cousin…or perhaps not.

"Excuse me, Mr. Spencer," Aunt Violet said as she quietly entered his study and shut the door behind her. "I'm sorry to bother you, but I must explain something."

Spencer had stood when she entered the room and he gestured to a chair. "Please sit. And call me Spencer."

"Thank you." She smoothed out her skirts, and Spencer noticed for the first time she was a beautiful lady and not as old as he originally believed. "I must apologize to you for my deception."

His heart sped up and his eyes locked with hers. "Deception?"

"Yes." She slid an envelope she held in her hand across his desk. "Please except my apologies."

After opening the envelope and finding a bank draft inside for the exact amount he paid for the townhouse, he raised his brows. "I don't understand?"

"I made the story up about my third husband running away with all our money." She raised her hand, seeing he was going to interrupt. "Please hear me out. He did run away with some money. Would have taken it all had some of it not been in my name only. And the house, well, it belonged to my second husband. He had no claim to it. I sold it and told Miranda we lost it."

"I'm confused."

"Yes, I imagine you are. If I didn't make up some desperate story, Miranda never would've left the country. I feared she would never marry, and when I die she would be all alone. I could not let that happen. So I did the only thing I could. I lied to get her to come to London and find a husband. Of course, I knew about yours and Miranda's past and I instigated an invitation to every function I knew you would be attending. How surprised I was for things to proceed as well as they did the first night you two reacquainted."

Spencer leaned forward, shaking his head in disbelief. "Let me understand. You have no need for my money? You did this for Miranda so she could find happiness and love?"

"Precisely."

"Forgive me if I take a moment to comprehend what this means."

"Please do."

"You do realize, when she finds out, she will be furious with you."

"Yes, well, that is why I need your promise not to tell her. She need never know."

"I'm not comfortable lying to my new wife."

"Come now, nephew, you need not lie. Just omit the truth."

"Put that way." He stood, came around the desk and bowed. "I am forever in your debt for bringing us together."

She flicked her wrist. "Nonsense. All I ask is you treat her with kindness and love. She deserves no less."

"True. And you can count on me."

Aunt Violet left him leaning against his desk with his heart pounding and his mouth hanging open at her confession. Perhaps she should confess to a priest because he could not give absolution for her sins. But he was indeed so thankful for them.

What a conniving aunt Miranda had. He had her undying respect and gratitude. Now, if only he could get his lovely new bride to fall in love with him again. It certainly was more attainable since they were married. He could woo her anytime day or night. Her aunt hinted at their past. Could he believe Miranda still had feelings for him?

That was, if she wasn't miffed at his desertion on their wedding night. Which made him wonder if she was upset and disappointed he didn't consummate their marriage? Perhaps she thought he didn't want her? His stomach twisted up in knots. No. She would never believe such an untruth, would she?

Bloody bugger, he needed to find her and clear the air.

Only when he inquired to her whereabouts, the housekeeper informed him she accompanied his sisters shopping on Bond Street, and they would be gone all day.

Great. As guilt burned a hole inside his body, his wife was out shopping.

❄

MIRANDA, after having a restless night sleep, found it hard to enjoy herself. Shopping on Bond Street would normally be something she would love. However, she found it hard to keep up with Liz and Mary as they visited one dressmaker, hat shop, and shoe shop after another. How much did they receive monthly in pin money? Because, if Miranda calculated all their purchases it totaled a very large sum.

She bought nothing. How much would Spencer allow her for monthly spending on such frivolous items? Her marriage, after only a day, seemed strained, and she wouldn't want to upset him by making purchases without his permission. Which made her eyes tear and her throat burn at the memory of him leaving her alone on their wedding night. What type of man did that? She'd lain in bed, broken-hearted and angry. When Liz and Mary asked if she wanted to go shopping, she'd jumped at the chance to get out of the house. Away from him.

Call her cowardly, but she'd even taken her breakfast in her room. Afraid she would see her husband and cry over her eggs and make a scene in front of his family. Not the way she wanted to start her marriage.

Now, at this very moment, when her body wanted nothing more than to crawl beneath the covers of her bed and sleep for two days straight, she found herself being hustled out the door of one establishment and into another.

"Let's go for ices at Gunter's," Liz, holding numerous packages, said.

"That sounds wonderful, I haven't had one in years." She could finally rest her weary body and sore feet since going home to bed anytime soon obviously wasn't an option. Liz and Mary were tireless shoppers.

As they exited the shop, the man who hadn't been far from her mind the entire day leaned against his phaeton with an intense look on his face which made her insides tighten.

"Ladies." He bowed and grinned. "I was hoping to persuade my dear wife to accompany me for a drive in the park."

"By all means," Liz said before Miranda could answer for herself. "Mary and I have one more stop to make before we go home. "If you happen to see Amesbury riding through the park without a care in the world, kindly tell him I'm still upset with him."

Obviously, it didn't matter whether she wanted to go for a ride with her husband or not. The decision had been made, and she found herself being helped into the vehicle by Spencer. "What was that about?" she asked once they were both seated, and he took the reins and urged the horses forward into Bond Street traffic.

"Edward Worthington, otherwise known as the Marquess of Amesbury, one of Wentworth's closest friends and Liz became friendly during the Season. I even believed he would offer for her. Then one day he didn't call. He didn't send flowers and a light extinguished from her eyes." He paused and spared her a quick glance full of concern. "Don't let her happy demeanor fool you. She has a broken heart and I'm at a loss as to how to help her."

"Have you tried talking to her or even Amesbury?"

"Yes and no. Lizzie won't tell me what happened. And I don't think it's my place to confront Amesbury?

"Why not? Since your father is no longer living, I would think you have every right to get involved."

"Perhaps if things don't improve between them, I will. In the meantime, I'll be available if she feels the need to confide in me. Of course, I blame myself as I should've paid more attention to what was going on around me. Instead I was giving all my undivided attention to Bella in hopes she would marry me instead of Myles."

"Oh." Her stomach dropped. "So the rumors are true?"

She'd known they were, but hearing it come from his lips made it all the more real. Her nerves were already stretched to the breaking point and his confessing only added to her tension. Not to mention the hit to her self-esteem making her more insecure where their marriage was concerned. For some reason, deep down inside her heart, she'd believed, perhaps not right away, but in the near distant future, their marriage would be real.

"Afraid so. Myles and Bella belong together and I knew it from the start. I was deluding myself into thinking I had a chance with her. She told me and never led me to believe otherwise." He paused and pulled the carriage off Rotten Row and down a narrow path. Turning toward her, he placed his free hand over hers. "Deep down inside I knew it never would be. You don't have to worry, I love Bella, but not that way."

Miranda didn't know what to say. Was he implying he loved her? Or reassuring her he didn't love Bella? Was she supposed to pretend she had no feelings for Spencer? Because clearly, after his snub last night, he'd made it perfectly clear he didn't want her.

No wonder she'd woken with an upset stomach today. "Thank you for clearing that up. You no longer love Bella." The words came out more harshly than she intended.

His eyes registered shock. "Not what I said, but close enough. Miranda." He lowered his voice and his eyes softened. "I want us to have a chance at a happy marriage. You must not hold whatever it was I did to you twelve years ago against me."

Her back straightened. "You know very well what you did." How could he not remember promising to ask her father for her hand and lying? Her hands began to tremble as well as the rest of her body.

"I beg to differ." He looked truly perplexed. *Why?* Then his eyes drifted across the way. "Bloody hell, are those storm clouds? We better make haste."

The moment they pulled up in front of Spencer House the clouds burst open, the wind kicked up, and rain pelted them to the point they were drenched by the time they entered the foyer.

Spencer gave orders to the butler to find Mrs. Noble and have baths readied for them both.

Miranda didn't know how she felt about their conversation being interrupted. Especially since she felt they were getting somewhere. Perhaps he would have explained why he didn't come for her all those years ago. Anything would have been better than what her imagination led her to believe. She remembered all too well the pain of being forgotten by Spencer. She had felt old and inadequate. She didn't want to live like that anymore. Yet here she was, one minute feeling hopeful in her relationship with Spencer and the next spiraling down in despair of ever having a true marriage. She didn't think she could take much more.

After her bath, her maid informed her that her husband requested her company in his study.

Standing outside his closed study door, she rested her hand on her stomach as butterflies fluttered around. *Would the family move out already.* And she chastised herself for being hopeful once again. Before she could knock she heard his deep voice. "Come in."

"How did you know I was outside?" she asked as she sat in a comfortable chair facing his desk.

"The soft sound of slippers on the wood floors."

"I see." She smoothed out her skirts to the pink and cream satin day dress. More to stall for time as the butterflies had only increased their flying velocity.

"I asked you here so we could continue our conversation without interruption. I believe I will have a glass of brandy. Would you care for some sherry?"

"No, thank you." She wanted to keep her wits about her.

After he settled back in his seat with his glass of amber liquid he looked at her with all seriousness. "I want you to know that I did not abandon you twelve years ago. I went to your house and spoke with your father. To my utter dismay, he refused my offer. Told me you never wanted to see me again and you were in love with another."

Her stomach plummeted. "You did? He did?" Her voice sounded strange to her ears.

"Yes."

"How do I know you're not lying to get into my good graces?" Where had those words come from? Never had she not trusted him before. Deep down inside, where her rational mind resided, she knew he told the truth. Except...it was his word only. Only her father said she loved another which wasn't true. Nor did she ever utter the words she never wanted to see him again. Her father had lied and refused Spencer's marriage proposal without consulting her.

"Now why would I not tell the truth? I was devastated by it. Why do you think I haven't married all these years?"

Her hands became the object of her fascination as she stared at them resting on her lap entwined together almost painfully. "Did my father say anything else? Give you another reason why he refused you?"

"Yes. Because of William and the rumors he killed Geoffrey and Katherine. He felt my family name was tarnished beyond repair." The pain in his voice and in his eyes was painful to bear. "That losing estates back to the crown was a better fate than marrying his only daughter into a murderous family."

"I see." Her throat and lungs burned. Her poor father.

What a dilemma he had had. Obviously, he felt strongly against her marrying into the Spencer family that he even made up the story about her loving another. What it must have cost him to refuse. Fortunately, her father did not lose his estates, although they lived like paupers. Since his death the title went to a distant cousin they never even knew existed.

How much he must have loved her, believing in the rumors and thinking he was keeping her safe. How they all suffered. Even Spencer. My God, what he must have gone through. All these years she had no idea he suffered right along with her.

When she found her voice she spoke quietly. "I'm terribly sorry for what my father said. I had no idea. I was led to believe you never called. My father said he hadn't seen you." She fought back tears threatening to spill but eventually gave up and let them trickle down her face. So many people had suffered from her father's choice. She wanted to hate him for his deceit, but she couldn't. He'd made those difficult decisions to protect her.

"Don't cry. It is in the past," Spencer consoled as he came around the desk, hunkered down, and took her hands in both of his. "Your father believed he did the right thing. He lied to protect you. How could he have known William didn't commit the crimes? If memory serves me, both your parents died several years later, and you moved to the country to be with your aunt. I should have sought you out then. I should not have given up. I should've know you didn't fall in love with another."

He brought her hands to his lips and kissed her knuckles. Without gloves separating them, the warmth from his lips sent heat sliding up her arms to curl around her heart until it was encased in soothing warmth.

"What I want to know is can you forgive me for not

fighting for you. For not pursuing you after your parents' death."

Hearing the anguish in his voice and viewing the desperation on his face startled her. "There is nothing to forgive. It is as much my fault as yours. I didn't have to run away. I could have stayed and confronted you. Except I thought you rejected me and hated me." She cried as a sob escaped.

Next thing she knew, he pulled her up. Folding her into his warm, comforting arms, he ran one hand up and down her back as he whispered, "Don't cry. All is right now. We are together. Married. The future is ours to make of it what we will. And please know, I could never hate you. I'm not capable of hating you. Anything but."

How could he be so forgiving for what her father had done? Could she, now that the truth was known, forgive her father? Yes, because he loved her and believed he was protecting her. "But all those wasted years. I understand what my father did was out of love and the need to protect me, but still he knew how much I loved you."

"They weren't wasted." He rubbed his cheek against the top of her hair and breathed in. "Besides, all that matters is now."

She inhaled and exhaled, willing her tears to stop. Her head lifted from his chest and she ventured a glance at him. Her heart melted at the concern on his face and in his beautiful, blue-green eyes. Leave it to Spencer to not have blue eyes or green, but a mixture of both. Eyes which presently were looking at her so intently she squirmed.

"I need to kiss you. May I?"

Words escaped her, so she nodded her head and his lips descended upon hers and it felt like coming home. Everything about the kiss was familiar. At first he took it slow. When his tongue ran across the seam of her lips she opened her mouth to him and moaned as he swept his tongue inside her mouth tasting her. *Why should he have all the fun?* She tangled her tongue with his and heard him moan as well as felt the vibration in his chest. His arms tightened around her waist, pulling her closer so their bodies molded together from head to toe. Her body melted against his, reveling at the muscle hardness of it. When she first felt his arousal pushing against her stomach she almost backed up in panic. But her mind calmed her down by telling her it was Spencer not Mr. Baker. Everything about being close to her husband was different from her aunt's third husband.

Eventually, needing air, she broke the kiss and rested her head against his chest once more. His heart pounding against her ear made her smile, knowing she was responsible for making it throb.

"I want you so desperately I can't think straight." The deep sound of Spencer's voice had her knees weakening.

"I want you too." And she did. She might be frightened to death about the sensual act, but she did so want him to make love to her. She'd waited a lifetime for this. Thought about it for most of her life. Dreamed about it many nights, causing her to awaken aroused and frustrated at how to make it go away or even to understand what was happening to her body. How to keep her heart from shattering on a daily basis for twelve lonely years.

"Do you think it scandalous if we retire to our chambers before dinner?"

His question surprised her and she giggled. *Giggled?* She couldn't recall ever doing that before. "We are newly married. What can be scandalous about that?"

"True indeed." He took her hand and while they strolled through the house and to the wing which housed their chambers, she struggled with the panic trying to overtake her.

How mortifying if she cast up her accounts on the hallway rug?

This was Spencer. The man who loved her. The man she loved. He would never hurt her. Never force her to do things she wasn't comfortable doing. But what would he say when he found her no longer a virgin?

Would he be angry?

"Relax." He leaned close to her ear and murmured, "I can feel the tension in your fingers, never mind radiating off your whole body. If you're not ready for this just say the words."

The words she needed to say would not come forth. What would he think of her if he knew the truth? Would he be revolted and disgusted? Not ever wanting to touch her, love her?

Once inside the room, she dropped his hand, walked toward the hearth and hugged herself, hoping to ward off the sudden chill taking over her mind as well as her body. She needed to win the battle because the last thing she wanted was to freeze Spencer out. But how to let him in? Let him into a truth about herself so horrifying she hated herself for it. Could hardly look in the mirror somedays. She knew what happened to her was not her fault, but the degradation and pain went deep, too deep to ignore. Even deeper than the hurt she had carried from Spencer's rejection.

"You're cold. Perhaps taking that ride in the park was a bad idea."

"No. It was perfect."

He grabbed the fireplace poker and stoked the embers until the flames licked up. "Here, let me warm you." He stood behind her and wrapped his arms around her waist, pulling her tight against him. "If you are having second thoughts. I understand."

She tried to relax, she really did. "No. It's your right."

"Damn it, Miranda." He dropped his arms and paced the room. "I am your husband. Not some brut from medieval times who ruts with his wife, then grunts and rolls off until he feels the itch again. I love you, have always loved you, and will until I take my last breath."

CHAPTER NINE

Did he have any idea how much those words meant to her? How much they moved her and almost made all her nightmares and fears dissolve? "I love you, too," she said through her tears. "Have since the first time I saw you. You were the only gentleman I saw at the ball that first night of my Season. Nobody else mattered now or then."

"Please let me make love to you? I need you."

He no longer paced the room but stood right in front of her. Never had she seen him look as though his life depended on her answer. So moved was she, it took several moments to find her voice. "You have no idea what those words mean to me." But she did. The love he had for her was written all over his face, in the depths of his eyes and in the cadence of his voice.

Was it enough to slay her demons? Only one way to find out. She took his hand and pulled him toward the four poster bed looming large in the middle of the room. Once there, she faulted and waited for Spencer to take the lead. Thankfully, he did. Even after all these years he still understood her.

Turning her around, he began undoing the pearl buttons

on the back of her dress. The brush of his fingers on her bare skin as he undid one button after another had heat curling low in her belly. As more buttons became undone the heat intensified. Her dress fell silently to the floor. Moments later, her chemise and then her pantaloons joined the satin heap pooling at her feet and she shivered.

"You are so beautiful," Spencer said as he kissed her neck and shoulder. "It was worth twelve years." Afraid to turn around and have him see her nakedness from the front, her feet stayed frozen to the thick Aubusson rug.

"I'll just divest myself of some clothing as well." With her eyes closed, she could hear the crinkling of him removing his coat, then waistcoat. The rustling as he untied his cravat and the sound of his shirt unbuttoning and being pulled over his head. She wanted so badly to see and feel his naked skin against hers.

"I believe I will sit on the edge of the bed and pull off my boots." Once again, she closed her eyes and heard, first one boot then the other hit the rug with a soft thud. More clothing noise as he no doubt unbuttoned the front placket of his breeches. For what seemed like an eternity, she waited for something to snap her eyes open. That something came in the clearing of Spencer's throat.

"Come here, my dear." Inhaling and exhaling for courage, she turned around and found the bed covers pulled down and Spencer's naked and aroused, body facing her.

So that's what a man looked like beneath his clothing. Oh, she could well imagine every man did not possess Spencer's hard lines, bulging muscles, and narrow waist. But they all did have that appendage protruding between their thighs. *Do not think about that yet.* Light brown hair dusted his chest. A darker line dipped low and surrounded his prominent erection. She swallowed the panic seeing it hard, large and looming toward her. *Stop looking at it.* Listening to her own advice, she raised her eyes and concentrated on the muscles rippling on his chest and arms and the grin on his smug face at her being caught looking at him.

"Come." He held out his hand and his face softened. "Do not be afraid of me. I will never hurt you."

Did he know? Surely not. He referred to her maidenhead and thinking it would cause her pain. She hesitated for a moment then climbed on the bed. Her hands were reaching for the coverlet at the same time Spencer pushed it aside and covered her body with his hard one.

His head dipped down, pressing his lips to hers in a kiss that conveyed how much he cherished her. She hoped she didn't disappoint him with her inexperience as he continued kissing her with the mind tingling kiss. Tingling that not only affected her head but other places on her body which seemed overly sensitized, warm, and moist.

Breaking the kiss, he whispered in her ear, "You have no idea how much I have dreamed about this moment. Almost every night for twelve long years."

Did she dare admit the truth to him? That she had as well. Although in her dreams they were always clothed. Which if they were making love, was odd. Even if her experience told her people could be nearly fully clothed and still perform the sex act. "Me too."

His groan upon hearing her reply was music to her ears. Then his mouth descended upon hers again and all thought vacated her mind.

After devouring her, drinking from her mouth, leaving her desperate for air and the room spinning around her, he broke the kiss. Her breathing was halted mid-inhale as his soft lips placed light, fairy wing kisses down her neck, across her collarbone and down to her breasts which were full and heavy. *An odd, but wonderful sensation*. When his hot tongue flicked across her nipple she arched up, her hands clung to his shoulders. Never had she experienced anything remotely resembling this. This need to pull him close and beg for something her body craved but her mind didn't comprehend.

"Do you like that?" He tongued her other nipple and she had the same reaction. Only this time she wanted to cross her legs at the sensations happening down there. At the wetness between her thighs.

Just as she was sinking more deeply into the bed and enjoying the attention he bestowed upon her breasts, he removed his mouth and her brain screamed, "No, stay." Then she gasped, "Oh my," as his mouth rained kisses down her stomach then laved her belly button with his tongue. Once again she had trouble keeping up as he nudged her thighs apart and he placed his mouth there. "Ohhhh," she moaned as her body responded by itself. Her hips rose off the bed seeking his mouth. Both hands fisted in his hair, non-too-gently, and she held on. Blissful, the sensations were so blissful until her mind intruded. *Who is this wanton woman? Is this what married couples do?*

"Stop thinking," he mumbled, breathlessly against her inner thigh. "I can hear the gears in your mind clicking. Feel. Just feel and let me love you with my mouth. Love you as you deserve to be loved for all time."

How could she resist when all she really wanted to do was open her legs wider, giving him better access to her womanhood. So she shut her mind down, spread her legs, closed her eyes, and let herself fall into the unknown. She trusted her husband. He loved her. He would never hurt her. Never make her do anything she didn't want to.

His tongue did sinful things to her, his fingers touched and caressed her everywhere, making her body heavy.

"Oh God," she breathed and squeezed her knees against his head. "I can't..."

"Let yourself go."

And somehow she did. A tightness coiled down low in her belly and traveled lower and lower still until her body trembled and the room exploded around her. All she recognized was heavy breathing coming from both of them. His body covered hers and he whispered, "Thank you," into her ear.

As his hard erection pushed against her womanhood, seeking entrance, everything slammed back into focus. Over-focused and over-sensitized and not in a good way. She tried to stop it from happening, she really did. But she no longer possessed her body or mind. She watched from above, no longer in control.

She slammed her eyes shut and wished to stay in the present with Spencer, the man she loved. But when she opened them again it wasn't her handsome husband she saw above her, it was him. Her aunt's husband, his face distorted and scrunched up as he grunted and groaned while he invaded her body, turning him into a monster.

"Stop," she screamed, only it didn't sound like her voice. Her hands came up and she shoved against the hard, wall of a chest. Her arms and legs began flailing about connecting with anything she could. But it was never enough, would never be enough to keep her safe. To keep the monster from violating her body against her will. To take the only thing she possessed that was truly hers to give...her innocence.

"What are you doing?" he bellowed. "Stop. It's me, Spencer. Look at my eyes, look at my face and tell me who Mr. Baker is?"

CHAPTER TEN

WHEN MIRANDA TOLD SPENCER ABOUT NOT KNOWING HE'D come to ask for her hand in marriage, mixed emotions churned inside his body. He wanted to be angry at her father. Wanted to hate him for what he'd done to both of them. Deep down inside he could not. How could he fault a parent for believing he was keeping his daughter safe? He'd made up the story of her being in love with another to protect her. People had honestly believed William had murdered Geoffrey and Katherine. The Spencer name no longer carried the respect and authority it once had. It hadn't been easy for his family to stay in London with their heads held high, but they had. It was a difficult and dark time for them. God knew, it almost killed William. Amelia saved him. If it wasn't for his grandmother and her stiff backbone insisting they stay in London because they had nothing to be ashamed of and nothing to hide, they would have all hidden in the country with William. Thank God for his grandmother.

If Amelia could save his cousin, he could save Miranda. Never had Spencer experienced such love and desire for anyone as he had minutes ago for his wife. He loved her and refused to lose her to her past. Whatever that may be.

When Miranda began screaming and hitting him, he tried to subdue her without injuring her. It proved to be a difficult task as she was stronger than he thought. Her fear had made her powerful. Several times she connected with his jaw and he believed he would sport a bruise tomorrow. He managed to keep her fingers away from his eyes and her feet from wounding his now flaccid manhood, but it wasn't easy.

Eventually, he convinced her it was him and he meant her no harm. Now she lay sobbing her heart out in his arms, and he battled between wanting to go and kill this Mr. Baker person or remain holding his broken wife in his arms. The answer was easy. Continue to hold and hopefully calm down Miranda. He murmured soft, loving and soothing words to her while his heart cracked wide open. His insides waged a war. Half of him wanted to know what happened to her, the other half did not. Not because finding out would ever make him feel differently about her. It would hurt Miranda to tell him and relive it all over again. Because even without her confiding in him, he knew what horrible event she'd lived through. His job now was to help her because she meant everything to him. If she suffered, he suffered.

"Do you want to tell me what happened?" He fought to keep his voice calm and even.

"No," she said between sobs.

"I'm here. I'm not going anywhere." And to prove it he held her tighter and willed his body to help her relax.

"I'm so ashamed," she cried out.

"Go on." Please God, give him the strength to listen and not upset her more. He had to remain calm in order to be helpful. This was about her, not him.

"My aunt's third husband is Mr. Baker. He is somewhat younger than she, although she didn't know it at the time she married him. Nor did Aunt Violet know what an accomplished liar he was."

Her whole body tensed up in his arms as she spoke, and he wished the conversation never needed to take place.

"After they were married for several months we found out he had no money and was stealing from us."

"The degenerate."

Her chest rose and fell as she breathed and then her body quivered from head to toe. "He took all of Aunties money and said he was traveling to America. We thought that would be the end of him, but that night he snuck into the house and came into my bedchamber."

Pausing, she wrapped her arms tighter around his waist. "I awoke to him opening the placket of his breeches. I froze. Didn't know what to do. I stared in horror as his body came down on top of mine and his hands shoved my night rail up around my waist."

"The bastard." The moment she panicked and said Mr. Baker's name, he'd known. Having the words fall from her lips intensified the horror for him. He supposed it did for her as well.

"I remember squeezing my eyes shut and my body going stiff as he covered me and pushed his...his...thing inside me and then pinning my body to the mattress while he bucked against me. The pain was unbearable. At one point he stopped moving, and I opened my eyes to see his face twisted up grotesquely. Then he climbed off me, buttoned up his breeches and thanked me for a most enjoyable evening and left."

Spencer's insides seethed with rage. Somehow, someway he would make the man pay for what he did to Miranda. He'd raped her and clearly she still suffered from her violation. Probably always would. How his heart broke for her.

"First and foremost, you have nothing to be ashamed

about. The man raped and violated you. He forced himself on you. Used brute force and strength to overtake you. Invaded your private bedroom and took his hate and anger out on you, an innocent."

He pulled away from her. "Look at me. I want to see your face." As anger seethed inside him, he fought to calm down for Miranda's sake.

She shook her head and refused to look him in the eye. "I can't."

"Yes, you can." He gently reached out and cradled her face in his hands and looked directly into her haunted, dark green eyes. "You have no need to hide from me. I want to help you."

"You can't." She cried and averted her gaze.

The thought of her giving up only made him push the issue.

"Let me try?"

"Why?"

"Oh, my dear, in case you haven't noticed, I love you and what hurts and torments you does the same to me as well."

Her eyes moved back to his and his insides clenched up at the shame and embarrassment he witnessed within their depths.

"You must think vile thoughts about me. Must be upset I'm not innocent."

"You *are* innocent." He had trouble keeping the rage from his voice, but when he saw her wince, he exhaled to regain control and softened his voice. "What happened to you didn't take away your innocence. He stole your virginity, but don't let him win by stealing who you are inside. Don't let him take away the wonderful, caring person you are in here." He touched her chest lightly with his fingers "Please don't let him win and ruin what we have. You deserve to be happy and loved."

"I don't know if I'm capable of it."

"Does your aunt know?"

"Yes. When I told her what he'd done she threatened to find him and cut off his...well...you understand. She said it was her fault. She'd seen him looking at me with lust and had done nothing. I wish I'd never told her. I caused her more pain and anguish, not to mention a boatload of guilt."

His insides relaxed a tad as Miranda's voice sounded more and more like herself. He could hear the strong, determined woman inside trying to find her way out. "Nonsense. What I want to know is did he ever board the ship to America?"

"I cannot say for certain. You don't think...?" Her eyes widened in alarm.

Damn it! He should have kept his mouth shut. She didn't need to worry that he would come back and rape her again. Not that the man would ever get past him. He'd die before he'd let her get hurt again.

"I'm quite convinced he left. He would be daft not too. You can bring charges against him if he stayed." Spencer planned on hiring a good acquaintance of his, Mr. Smythe, the best Bow Street Runner that ever existed. If the man resided in England he would be found. If he went across the pond to America, then good riddance. Hopefully, he'd find himself wandering the American mid-west and meet an Indian who scalped him. The vision had Spencer's body trembling. It would be a fitting way for him to die.

"I'm sorry you had to go through that. But please believe me that most men are not like him. We would never force ourselves on a lady. I will never force myself on you. We can spend the nights together in bed sleeping and nothing else until you are ready." And he meant it from the bottom of his heart. Being with her in any capacity was better than existing without her. He'd done that and didn't relish repeating it.

❄

WHAT DID she ever do to deserve this kind, considerate, and caring man? How shocked he must have been when she started screaming and hitting and kicking him. She was utterly mortified at her behavior toward the man who loved her. A man who had every right to her body.

Did he regret marrying her? She didn't think so. But perhaps she should have told him the truth before their wedding day. Let him make the decision to marry her or not. Instead she took the decision away from him.

"If it's to your liking, you can have our marriage annulled." It nearly tore her heart apart to say the words, but she had to know he still wanted her damaged and all.

His gentle hands cupped her face again. "Never. You will never get rid of me. That is unless...it is what you desire?"

The panic and sadness in his eyes caused a stabbing pain inside her chest. "No. It's not what I want. I suppose I needed your reassurance."

"You have it and more."

She moved away, sat up, and tucked the covers beneath her arms covering up her breasts. "Thank you."

"Thank you for what?"

"For being so understanding. For being the same wonderful man I fell in love with when I was seventeen. For not hating me for what my father did to you. And for forgiving me for deceiving you into marrying a damaged woman."

His arm wrapped around her shoulders as he pulled her close against his side, and her insides soothed. "First, your father hurt both of us. And I already told you I understand why he did it. He thought he was doing what was best for you. Let us put it behind us and concentrate on today and the future." He kissed the top of her head. "As for you thinking you are damaged, you're far from it. It tears my heart apart to hear you call yourself that."

Closing her eyes she breathed in his male scent of sandal-wood and something uniquely his and gathered strength.

"You must be tired, why don't you lie back and rest." His lips brushed the side of her temple. "I have something I need to take care of and then I'll return."

When he left the bed and room, the warmth went with him and she burrowed beneath the covers, willing her mind to go blank so she could sleep. She was beyond exhausted, both physically and mentally. Things always looked more promising when she was well rested. The morning would bring sunshine and with it hope. At least she prayed it did

SPENCER CLOSED the door to their bedchamber and leaned his forehead against it to control the trembling of his body. Now that he was alone, he could fall apart and let the horror Miranda lived through penetrate his mind. His poor wife going through something so vile and hateful, degrading and hurtful. No woman should ever be treated so badly no matter where she came from. It took immense self-control not to pound the door with his fists to get out the anger and rage boiling up inside him.

Tears blurring his vision, he stumbled blindly through the hall, descended the stairs, and didn't feel somewhat in control until he sat behind his desk and began penning notes to both Smythe and William. He became annoyed with himself for having to keep stopping and swiping away his tears. Tears he cried for Miranda. Finally he could see enough to finish penning the letters, and he rang the butler and instructed him to send off the missives immediately. It was the middle of the night, but he didn't care. They needed to be sent.

Once the notes were en route, he sat with a glass of whiskey, hoping to numb his mind of the horrors it kept picturing. He witnessed Miranda being raped by a faceless man. Was this what she went through every single day of her life since that awful event? Did she relive the violation and degrading ordeal every night when she slept in her dreams?

After two drinks he went to his room. Even though he was afraid to sleep, afraid of the dreams that would visit him, he went and climbed in bed with his wife. She appeared deeply asleep as she didn't even stir when his weight dipped the bed. Nor when he wrapped an arm beneath her back and pulled her close. All she did was sigh and snuggle deep into his body as if she knew he was there. As if she slept with him every night instead of this being the first. Somehow she knew he wasn't a danger.

Having her warm, pliant body against his, slowed down his heart and breathing to a normal cadence. Eventually his eyes began to droop until finally they closed for good and he slept.

Somewhere in his subconscious mind he heard whimpering and soft crying. Then something changed and he heard screaming and something shoved against him. Consciousness slammed into him, and he realized Miranda was screaming and pushing against him while repeating the words, "No," over and over again.

"Easy, my love, it's me, Spencer. You're safe. No one can harm you now. It was only a nightmare, not real. I'm here. You are safe. Baker can never hurt you again."

Her body trembled against his, and he pulled the covers up high. Her skin was cold and damp. "Go back to sleep. I'll keep your nightmares away."

He could almost feel her mouth quirk up into a smile. "No one can keep my nightmares away, but you can help. You are helping. Usually, Auntie comes running down the hall to shake me awake when I dream of it. I don't know what I would've done without her all this time. Do you know she is only ten years older than me? More like my older sister than my aunt."

"When you first mentioned you went to live with your aunt after your parents' deaths, I pictured a matron of advanced years. If you don't think she'll mind me asking, what happened to her first two husbands?"

When her breathing slowed to normal and her body stopped trembling he sighed with relief. "Her first husband was a wealthy vicar. I know what you are thinking, how can a vicar be wealthy? Well, I have no answer to that except he left my aunt quite a bit of money when he died choking on fatty meat."

"How odd, although not uncommon."

"Yes, well. Since I never met him I have no opinion of him at all. Her second husband was a wealthy landowner. I believe she loved him deeply. Unfortunately, not two years after their marriage, he somehow managed to fall down their well and drown. It took days for him to be found. My poor aunt was increasing at the time and lost the baby. I met him only once, but he seemed a good man. I don't know why my aunt married Mr. Baker except to say she was lonely, living in the country, and there aren't many eligible men there."

"How heartbreaking to go through two tragedies and end up married to a lying, cheating, degenerate," he said.

"Yes, indeed."

He kissed the top of her head. "Do you think you're ready to sleep now? I'm embarrassed to admit my eyes are drooping."

She moved her hand to cover his heart and he held his breath. Afraid if he made a sound or moved she'd take it away. She didn't.

"I'm sleepy. After I experience one of those nightmares, I'm either wound up and afraid to go back to sleep or so physically and mentally drained I fall asleep almost immediately. Tonight, with you here with me, I can sleep. Thank you for talking to me and pulling me out of it."

"Anytime." He kissed the top of her head again. "Good night."

"Good night," she whispered back.

He covered her hand, the one resting on his chest, with one of his and fell asleep feeling content and happy for the very first time in his entire life.

CHAPTER ELEVEN

Not long after breakfast, the butler announced that Mr. Smythe and Bridgeton had arrived. Spencer found them both waiting for him in the gloom of his study. Though the fire blazed in the hearth, it could not combat the dreary rainy day.

"What is so important you had me up tossing and turning all night after receiving your note at the ungodly hour of two?" Bridgeton asked as he leaned forward in his seat, resting his hands on his thighs.

Smythe said nothing, just raised his brows in silent question.

"Smythe, I would like to hire you to find someone. I know I don't have to tell you what I say stays between the three of us. I don't want my wife or her aunt to worry that this will get out."

"For bloody sakes, tell us before I go crazy," William said, raking his hand through his hair.

"The name of the man I want you to find is a Mr. Henry Baker of Manchester. At least that is where he said he was from. It could be a lie. All I know is he told Miranda's Aunt Violet, he was from there."

"What is this man to them?" Smythe asked as he made notes in a small book with a sharpened piece of coal.

Spencer closed his eyes and wished it wasn't too early to partake in something strong to drink. "He is married to Miranda's aunt. He lied about having money and began to steal from them. When Mrs. Baker found out she threw him out. He came back that night and attacked Miranda." He inhaled shakily and leaned back against his chair. Uttering the words out loud somehow made it all the more real.

"Attacked as in how?" This question came from his cousin who barely suppressed his anger.

Spencer's eyes flicked from his cousin to Smythe, back to William. "He raped her."

William's fist came crashing down on the desktop. "The bloody bastard!"

"Can you tell me anything else about this man?" Smythe said, looking none too pleased.

"He was supposed to leave on a ship to America. They don't know if he did."

"I'll get right on it." Smythe stood up and paused at the door. "What do I do when I find him?"

"Give me his whereabouts and I'll take it from there."

"Are you out of your mind," William bellowed. "You are normally not a violent man, but I can see something unsettling in your eyes. Let Smythe handle it. If he's still in England, let him personally escort him aboard a ship not to America, but on a penal ship to New South Wales. He deserves to live amongst criminals."

"Listen to your cousin," Smythe interjected. "He speaks wisely."

He wanted to tell Smythe to go to hell, but he knew the

man spoke sensibly. "Very well, but keep me abreast of the situation."

After Smythe left, Spencer faced William and thought the hell with it, he needed a brandy. He held up the decanter, "Care for a drink or two or three?"

"One and then I am going home to hug my wife and daughter."

Spencer thought back to William's twelve years of solitude by choice. "Did you ever think during those years of being alone and in mourning, you would ever find yourself married and happy?"

William grinned over the rim of his tumbler. "Never, I thought I would die alone and miserable."

"Well, I am personally glad you didn't. I like to think God sent Amelia to you and you to her. Otherwise, you both would have withered and died an early death."

William chuckled. "Me first, no doubt, as I'm nearly twice her age."

"Precisely."

"Before I take my leave, please tell me how Miranda is? And am I allowed to share this with Amelia?"

"She is traumatized. It happened two months ago. My instincts tell me to hunt the bastard down, string him up and cut out his entrails, then slice off his cock and stuff it in his mouth."

William cleared his throat. "That bloodthirsty?"

"You have no idea what it was like seeing her panic while we were..." He cleared his throat. "Anyway, I believe she is strong and will get over this eventually. Meanwhile, if Baker shows up looking for them before Smythe finds him, Aunt Violet promised to cut off his cock as well. I am not the only bloodthirsty one in the family."

"Nice imaging. I'm going to have nightmares tonight and fix a metal bowl over my..."

"Amelia will get a good laugh at that."

"Seriously, what can we do?"

"Nothing for now, but when Smythe finds him, I might need you to lock me up so I don't go after him."

William stood. "You can count on me for whatever you need."

Left alone with his wayward thoughts had Spencer reaching for the decanter again, then pausing and thinking better of it. Miranda didn't need an inebriated husband on her hands. Instead he rang the bell and ordered his horse to be saddled. He needed a good, fast, long ride to clear his head before he faced his wife. If she saw the turmoil and bloodlust in his eyes it would worry her. Something he never wanted to do.

He wanted his wife happy, without a care in the world besides what gown to wear to the next ball.

DURING AFTERNOON TEA with Liz and Mary, Miranda wondered where the rest of the family had gotten off too, including her husband. Yes, she received word he went riding, but that was hours ago. Was he staying away from her because of what happened? Oh dear, her stomach knotted up at the thought.

"What has you frowning so?" Liz asked as she took a nibble of a biscuit that looked positively divine.

Unfortunately, she had no appetite. Delicious looking biscuit or not. "Sorry, I was thinking." Since she didn't want to dwell on her troubles, she changed the subject. "So tell me, is there a special man who has caught either of yours eyes?"

Mary blushed and Liz scowled. Oh dear, she'd forgotten about Amesbury so she focused on Mary.

"By the way you are blushing, I think you met someone Mary."

"Well. There is one gentleman who caught my eye, although I don't think he knows I'm alive. I never danced with him nor spoke to him. Not once."

"I'm sorry." She truly was. Unrequited love was painful. "Do you mind me asking who it is?"

Before she could answer Liz said, "The Marquess of Thorsten."

"Liz," Mary huffed. "How did you know? I never told you."

"Do you think I don't have eyes? Every time he attends the same function as us you stare at him. It is hard not to notice."

Mary gasped, covered her mouth with her hand, and cried out, "Oh my God, do you think he noticed?"

"No," Liz said quickly. "If he did, no doubt he would have approached you, or Spencer."

"Perhaps when the new Season begins he will come back to town. I have no doubt he is busy with his estates since he'd only inherited the title right before the previous Season."

"No doubt," Miranda said, hoping and praying this marquess noticed Mary. She was a rare beauty. Totally the opposite of Liz and Spencer in looks. Mary had milky white, flawless skin, thick wavy blonde hair, and a quiet demeanor. Any man who didn't notice Mary was blind. She was everything London men supposedly wanted. Quiet, polite, and biddable in a good way. Not like Liz and herself who were outspoken and not at all docile.

Miranda remembered Amesbury, although he didn't possess his title twelve years ago. She did remember him, Wentworth, and Northborough having the reputation of rakehells. My, had times changed. Two out of three were married and to strong women. Hopefully, Liz would get her man because when Amesbury's name came up, she looked positively dejected and heartbroken.

How she remembered those feelings well, and she wouldn't wish them on her worst enemy.

"Is there anything I can do to help you with Amesbury?"

Liz crossed her arms and glared at her. Then she sighed and shook her head. "I'm sorry. I'm not angry at you. I'm hurt and angry at him. Everything was fine with us. Progressing nicely." She paused, glanced around, leaned forward and lowered her voice, even though only the three of them occupied the drawing room at present. "Don't tell my brother, he held me real close one night and kissed me…using…his tongue."

"Ewe. That disgusting," Mary said, making a face.

Miranda responded before Liz could. "It may sound disgusting, but trust me, it is far from it. If you are kissing the right man, that is."

"It is not disgusting," Liz huffed. "Someday you will find out on your own. Perhaps your marquess will kiss you and put his tongue inside your mouth."

"Never." This time Mary began laughing. "Truly, people kiss with tongues. I had no idea."

All three of them laughed and Miranda hoped Mary didn't go and kiss the first gentleman she saw to test the disgusting tongue theory. She also hoped Amesbury came to his senses and called upon Liz soon.

"What is so funny?" Spencer asked as he entered the drawing room, still in his riding clothes, and Miranda could not help but admire his physique in his tight buff breeches and cropped brown riding jacket.

"Nothing," Liz said with a blush. "We were just discussing women issues."

"Oh," Spencer said with a grimace. "Please don't talk about such things when I'm around."

To change the subject Miranda asked, "How was your ride?"

"Long." He sat in a chair facing the three of them resting on the settee. "But I needed to clear my head."

When Liz and Mary looked at him and spoke at the same time Miranda cringed. "Why?" They both asked.

"Nothing that concerns you two."

Thank goodness the butler took that moment to announce a visitor. Miranda didn't want to think about what happened last night or why Spencer needed to clear his head. Even though he professed his love for her and he didn't want an annulment, she still had reservations. How long would he feel that way if she could not bring herself to perform her wifely duties?

"The Marquess of Amesbury," the butler announced surprising Miranda, along with Liz, who blushed and Mary who looked as though she would burst out laughing at any moment. This should be interesting, she mused.

"Amesbury." Spencer stood and shook his hand. "Nice to see you. I'd like to present my wife, Miranda."

"Miranda, this is the Marquess of Amesbury."

"It is a pleasure to finally meet the lady who stole Spencer's heart." Amesbury bowed.

Miranda smiled. "Such flattery, Amesbury. Please have a seat next to Lady Elizabeth." She indicated the seat on the settee she just vacated and ignored the scowl Liz sent as she took the chair next to her husband's.

"So tell me, Amesbury, how long have you known my husband?"

"I've known him for years, but not until the past year did he and I become friends. When Bridgeton came to London in pursuit of Lady Amelia, Bridgeton and Spencer pushed themselves into our small circle of friends."

The sound of her husband's laughter was music to her ears.

"You must admit that our friendship brought a certain amusement to your otherwise staid group."

Now Amesbury laughed. Not quite music to her ears, but she was convinced it was to Liz's. "Amusement, that is putting attempted murder, loss of memory, and Newgate in another light. Although, you can be entertaining at times."

"You do realize insulting me will not help your chances with my dear sister who is staring daggers at me right now."

"Spencer!" Liz chastised, her cheeks turning red.

"Please accept my apologies, dear sister. Perhaps a change in topic is warranted. How is the weather Amesbury?"

The five of them laughed. "I see what you mean by entertaining," Miranda said. "My husband can be quite amusing at times."

"Not nearly as amusing as Amesbury can be. Or so I have heard." This was from Mary and all eyes fell on her. "What? Did I say something inappropriate?"

Amesbury looked uncomfortable as he tugged on his cravat, and Miranda felt sorry for him.

"My dear sister," Liz said looking wide eyed at Mary, "does not know what she is talking about."

"Yes I do. We were just laughing and talking about Amesbury right before he came."

Poor Amesbury. Now he looked as though he was unable to breathe, his face had turned beet red. A pity because he was extremely handsome. Not as handsome as her husband, of course.

Liz stood and glared at Mary. "Thanks. That was a big help." And she left the room without looking at anyone or begging her leave.

Spencer appeared at a loss for words and he looked at Miranda for help.

"I must apologize for Elizabeth. Right before you came she admitted to having an upset stomach. I'm sure she will be right as rain in no time." Miranda didn't know what to say to ease Amesbury's pained and embarrassed look. "Please feel free to call on Elizabeth tomorrow. I'm quite convinced she will be much better."

"Thank you."

After Amesbury left Spencer said, "Well, that was awkward. Does someone want to tell me what just happened?"

"Right before you joined us," Mary began, "Liz was telling us about her and Amesbury—"

"Nothing," Miranda interrupted. "She was telling us—"

Spencer held up his hand, frowned and shook his head. "Don't tell me. I don't want to know.

BRIDGETON FOUND his bride in the library cozied up in a chair with a book in front of the warm hearth. "I found you." He sank into the matching chair beside her and reached for her hand which she took.

"You left early this morning. The butler said you received a message from Spencer late last night. I do hope nothing is amiss?"

"Yes. Something is amiss all right." He exhaled deeply. "Spencer said I could confide in you. But you must promise not to tell anyone. Let Miranda share with the others if she so chooses. If what I have to say gets out Miranda would be mortified.

"Oh my, you make it sound scandalous."

"It is. Trust me, it is. Soon before she arrived in London her aunt's third husband raped her."

Gasps came from Amelia. "He...never mind. Don't say it again. How terrible. Where is he now?"

"That's just it. Spencer wants to find him and kill him. Not that I can blame him. I'd do the same if someone did that to you. But I don't think he's thinking rationally. And God knows I'm an expert on irrational behavior."

"Is Smythe on the case?"

"Of course. Between our families the man has more work than he can handle. We may as well start putting him on our invite list. He's here often enough."

"He is a rather handsome and charming young man. Perhaps one of Myles's sisters might consider him?"

"The *ton* would be scandalized at one of their members, the daughter of an earl no less, marrying a lowly working class citizen. I know Myles would approve. He likes and respects the man. Perhaps it's possible." William squeezed her hand.

"What is he going to do when he finds this...I can't call him a man, because he isn't."

"If he's still in England he will be escorted to a ship setting sale for New South Wales. If he cannot be found, he is likely in America. Hopefully, he died a horrendous death on the crossing."

"I sincerely hope so." Amelia squeezed his hand back. "Did you see Miranda since she told Spencer? Should I go and call on her this afternoon?"

"I don't know if he told her he shared the news with me and me with you? Until she mentions something, perhaps we should keep quiet. But by all means, we can call this afternoon. It would keep my mind off what was said between Spencer and myself this morning. But tell me my love, how you are feeling?"

"Fine...Oh." Amelia placed his hand on her increasing belly. "The baby moved. Can you feel him?"

"Yes." He smiled. "You, my dear wife, have made me the happiest man in all of England. I never thought..."

"I know. I never thought either. We both received a

second chance at happiness, life, and love. And we must not waste a moment of it. Geoffrey, Katherine, and Captain Rycroft are watching us from heaven. Their prayers as well as ours have come true."

"Has anyone told you, you are wise beyond your years?"

"Only you." She glowed."

"I mean it."

"I know. If you don't mind, I'm going to spend time in the nursery with Olivia before we leave."

"In case I don't tell you often enough, you are a wonderful mother."

"Thank you."

Before she exited the library, he pulled her up against his body and kissed her senseless.

CHAPTER TWELVE

"THE EARL AND COUNTESS OF BRIDGETON," ANNOUNCED the butler shortly after Amesbury took his leave.

The conversation went on and on around the room, and Miranda had a hard time keeping up with all the different topics. Eventually, she excused herself and went to stand in front of the hearth to clear her suddenly muddled mind.

"Do you mind if I join you?" asked Amelia, her new cousin-in-law.

"No, please do."

"How is our Spencer? He seems happy and content since the wedding?"

"He is. As am I."

"You have no idea how relieved William and I are that you found each other again. I think William gave up ever thinking his cousin would settle down and marry. Of course, he didn't know about the fact that Spencer still loved you for all these years."

"Bridgeton is one to talk. Did he not spend twelve years ignoring Spencer's attempts to speak to him, reason with him?"

Amelia smiled and her beauty startled Miranda. "True. William believes I saved him, and I believe he saved me and Olivia."

"I know Bridgeton's story. Well, I get the feeling I only know a tiny bit of it, but I'm fine with that. I don't, however, know anything about why you would think he saved you and Olivia? I can deduce your previous husband passed."

Amelia sighed. "Actually, I was never married. Please do not think me a horrible person. Captain Rycroft, my fiancé, and I were in love. It only happened once a month before our wedding. Who knew he would die a senight before our nuptials in a hunting accident."

"Oh, Amelia, I'm so sorry. How terribly sad for you." Miranda couldn't fathom what she went through. "If you don't mind me asking, how did you keep Olivia a secret from the gossips of the *ton*?"

"That wasn't easy. I went to America where Sebastian was living at the time. He and I came back when Olivia was a year old. We pretended my ladies maid was her mother. There was gossip, but nobody had any proof."

"It always comes down to gossip."

"When William and I fell in love, Wentworth would not allow him to court me. He still had the reputation of being a murderer. I was briefly engaged to the Duke of Yarmouth who, and please keep this to yourself, tried to force himself on me. By the grace of God, William had followed us into the gardens and pulled him off me. After that we eloped to Gretna Green."

As soon as the shock of hearing Amelia had almost been raped dissipated, she said, "Gretna Green. How romantic."

"Yes, well, we didn't make it. Emma, Bella, Wentworth, and Sebastian caught up with us. My brother finally gave his consent and we married at my family's country estate."

"Still, how very romantic. I can see why you think he saved you from a life of heartbreak. But him..."

"You know the story about his brother and sister-in-law's death?"

"Yes."

"And that he was blamed?"

"Yes."

"But there is more. After we married, Sir Phillip Trenton, Katherine's brother tried to drown me in the same stream he killed Katherine in."

She gasped and brought her hand to her throat. "Ohhh, how frightening."

"What made things worse was when I regained consciousness, I went back nearly three years to when Captain Rycroft still lived. I didn't remember ever meeting William, never mind marrying him."

"Dear me."

"Wentworth had him thrown in Newgate. Eventually, the truth came out, but it took a while."

"Now I see." And she did. Amelia and Bridgeton both deserved to have love and happiness. Thank God they found each other.

"There is more. During the opening of Waterloo Bridge, our boat was rammed and I fell into the Thames. Once again, Sir Phillip tried to kill me. William, Sebastian, and Wentworth rescued me. Finally William's name was cleared and he could hold his head up high again."

"That's an amazing story. I already held you both in high esteem, but it is even higher now."

"Thank you."

Miranda took a deep breath for courage. If Amelia could share her story, she could as well. "Can I tell you something in confidence?"

"Yes."

"I was raped by my aunt's husband two months ago."

"I...oh...I'm so sorry." Amelia looked completely shocked by her words. No doubt she looked like this moments ago when Amelia shared her own tragic story.

"What happened?"

Miranda went on to explain everything and the heavy burden of carrying such a secret lessened each time she shared it. First her aunt, then Spencer and now Amelia. She knew Amelia would understand after her own brush with rape.

Amelia turned and hugged her close and whispered in her ear, "We are kindred spirits."

Miranda hugged her back. "Thank you. I feel it too."

Amelia turned and looked at William and Spencer who were laughing. "Our husbands are handsome devils. We are so fortunate to have captured their hearts."

She had to agree. "We are indeed."

SPENCER SAT in his study more or less staring into his glass of brandy. A senight had gone by since Miranda told him about being raped, and he still didn't know how to help her. Did she want him physically comforting her or was being in a man's arms too much to bear? Whenever he spent time with her, all he wanted to do was ease her burdens and take them upon himself. If only that were possible. Seeing her haunted eyes during the day and waking to her nightly nightmares tore at his heart. He would do anything to take her pain and anguish away.

Unfortunately, he'd yet to hear from Smythe on Baker's whereabouts, and the days crawled by waiting for any tiny morsel of news.

"A gentleman is here to see you," his butler announced

with an annoyed look on his face. "He wouldn't divulge his name."

"Thank you. See him to the burgundy drawing room and stay with him until I arrive."

"Yes."

Intrigued as to who his visitor could be, he vacated his study, walked down the hall and into the small drawing room they seldom used because it faced north and tended to be dark and cold. Perfect for meeting his mysterious stranger.

"May I help you?" Spencer asked as he walked into the room and looked the man over from head to toe. Not very tall, a little too thin, but otherwise dressed respectably enough.

""Yes, you may."

"Do I know you?" The hairs on the back of his neck stood up, and a chill crept up his spine.

"We have never been formally introduced, but I am Mr. Henry Baker, Lady Violet's husband. Several close acquaintances of mine have informed me that my wife is staying here. I'd like to see her if you don't mind."

"Mind?" Spencer saw red flames shooting out of his very own eyes, and his body shook from the inside out. Rage, like he'd never known existed, slammed into him. Before he comprehended he'd moved, he punched the man in the nose, ignoring the pain that exploded in knuckles. He congratulated himself when he heard the recognizable sound of breaking bone.

"What the bloody hell do you think you're doing," yelled Baker. "You broke my nose. Are you out of your mind?"

Spencer watched with satisfaction as Baker removed a handkerchief from his pocket and tried to stop the rush of blood escaping his nostrils. He'd need something more than that little square of white linen.

"More important a question to ask is, are you an idiot for

coming into my home and acting like nothing happened between you and my wife?"

"Your wife?" the man asked in a nasally voice. And Spencer enjoyed the sight of his eyes beginning to swell and bruises appearing in the circles beneath them.

"Yes, Miranda, my wife." Spencer planted his body directly in front of Baker and leaned close. "You do remember her, don't you? But more importantly, she told me everything."

Baker backed up as fear flashed in his eyes. Then he made a most startling transformation. His back straightened and his features turned hard. "Well, well, well, this is even better. Perhaps you wouldn't mind relieving yourself of some pound sterling. Otherwise, I will shout out to the *ton* that Miranda seduced me while her aunt and I took pity on her by putting a roof over her head and food in her belly. That she is nothing more than a common whore. She will be ruined—you will be ruined."

Strangled cries from the hall bombarded his ears. Spencer's heart stopped, knowing the sounds came from his wife. His hand curled around Baker's throat, and he backed him up against the wall and squeezed. "You will do no such thing. I have the means and know how to make you disappear. Bribing guards in Newgate to make people vanish without a trace is something that occurs every day. How would you like to live the remainder of your numbered days in the sewers of hell...or worse?"

When Baker's lips tinged blue, he released his grip and the man fell forward onto all fours choking and sucking in air.

Spencer walked to the door and came face to face with not only Miranda, but Violet as they hugged each other. How much had they heard?

The sound of Miranda crying tore at his insides, and he almost turned around and finished what he started. They could dispose of the body and nobody would be the wiser. He highly doubted anyone would go looking for the scum of the London sewers. But deep down, Spencer could never take another life, no matter how much the person deserved to die. Letting Smythe deal with Baker was the right thing.

When Violet saw him, she pulled away from Miranda, put on a brave face and said, "If you will permit it, I would like a word in private with my husband."

"Be my guest." He pulled Miranda into his arms and gently rubbed her back. "Easy my dear. He can't hurt you. I will never let him or anyone else hurt you."

Between sobs she said," I know. It was just a shock to first hear his voice then to glimpse his face through the opening in the door. I thought Auntie would faint dead away at my feet when she heard him. Why is he here?"

"I'll explain all, but first I need to know you are fine?"

"I am. Or I will be now that I have a knight in shining armor looking out for me. Who knew you could be so gallant."

"Are you jesting?"

"I need too. Otherwise I might faint and land at your feet." She leaned back and looked right into his eyes and all the air escaped from his lungs. "Please tell me why he is here?" Her sad, pleading eyes nearly crippled him.

He stepped back, careful to keep one hand on her hip for support in case she needed it. His other hand clawed through his hair. "I'm not sure of the original reason. He said he heard his wife was staying here, and he wanted to see her. No doubt to try and squeeze her for more money. When I explained we were married he changed his mind and demanded money from me. He threatened to expose and ruin you in the eyes of society by lying about you."

"Yes, well, actually, I did hear him call me a...a...whore," she choked out."

"It is my understanding, and from experience, people desperate for funds will do or say anything to get what they think they deserve. He probably believes he's entitled to money."

"Why would he think that?"

"He is without compassion and morals. Come." He held out his hand. "Let us check on your aunt?"

The moment they stepped into the drawing room, Spencer saw Violet's hand rise up and slap Baker on the cheek. The sound of the smack reverberated in the small room. *Good for you, Violet.*

Baker's head snapped back at the contact. When all was over, he stared at her with pure hatred in his eyes. So much hatred that Spencer cringed, and he wondered how Violet could have married the man. Was he that good an actor he had her fooled?

"Well, since I obviously will not get what I came for, I will be off."

"Not so fast," Smythe said from the open doorway. "Your butler sent word to me the second he ascertained who your uninvited guest was."

"Thank you," Spencer said first to his butler then to Smythe. Then he addressed Miranda and her aunt. "Perhaps you two would like some tea in the family drawing room while Smythe and I take care of this unwanted business."

Once the ladies left, Spencer shut the door, ordered Baker to sit and turned the room over to the Bow Street Runner.

"Mr. Baker, my name is Robert Smythe and I'm the head of the Bow Street Runners. You have been accused of several serious crimes. Crimes which could have you put to death, or even worse, leave you to rot in Newgate. Prisoners have a way of being forgotten down in the dark bowels of hell. Dying of starvation is a slow and painful death. That is, if disease doesn't get you first."

"You have no right."

"I have every right. But you have an alternative. Instead of Newgate, where the guards are as corrupt as the prisoners, and all it takes is a small amount of coin to make things happen to one's advantage, you can board a ship to New South Wales. I'll be kind and not sign you to a penal colony. You can live free there."

"Those are my only choices?"

"Yes, pick one now. I'm a very busy man and so is Mr. Spencer. Make it quick before I give in to Mr. Spencer's wishes and turn you over to him. Trust me, you do not want that."

"Fine, put me on a ship."

"Before Smythe escorts you from my home." Spencer bent down and got close to Baker's face. "Let me be perfectly clear in explaining what will happen to you if you ever step one foot on English soil again. You will not be treated with such civility. If I ever glimpse your face again, I will end your pathetic existence where you stand." He rose, crossed his arms on his chest, and rocked back on his heels. "Do you understand?"

"I'm not a simpleton."

"I beg to differ. Get him out of my sight, Smythe,"

Left alone in the dark room, Spencer paced from one wall to the next while his fingers yanked his hair. It was either that or he would start throwing objects around or yelling from the top of his lungs, his frustration was that high. Part of him wanted to do just that, but the rational part of him didn't want to cause Miranda or Violet any more anguish. They certainly didn't need him sliding down into insanity, even temporarily, to appease his temper. He proceeded to sit in front of the cold hearth inhaling and exhaling, trying to slow the thundering of his heartbeat before it exploded out of his chest. When he first realized who Baker was, he'd frightened himself with his own hatred of the man. Never had he experienced pure, raw, rage. His emotions nearly spiraling out of control. It was a good thing he noticed Miranda in the hall when he had, otherwise he might have done something he'd regret for the rest of his life.

He could only imagine what Miranda went through when she realized Baker was inside her home. Invading the peace and safety of her own domain. Now that the bastard was taken care of, it was time to concentrate of healing Miranda. Spencer would do anything for her. She meant everything to him, and the thought of her going through what she did nearly paralyzed him with anguish. He needed to be strong, calm, and loving for her sake.

WHEN MIRANDA and her aunt were walking arm and arm down the hall in the direction of the family drawing room for afternoon tea, and the eerie sound of Baker's voice traveled to her ears, she thought she would be sick.

Never had she believed hearing his voice again would tumble her right back to that night. His deep timber traveled in her ear throughout her entire body and out the other ear leaving a wake of destruction behind. Thank God Auntie grabbed her when she had or she would've hit the floor hard.

She never thought she'd hear him again. Hear the voice that snuck into her mind while she slept at night and terrorized her to the point of waking her up and then keeping her awake, afraid to fall back to sleep. Afraid to sleep because the voice would find her again.

When she'd caught sight of him between the open cracks of the door and heard him refer to her as a whore, she'd decided at that exact moment to not let him win. What he did to her was traumatic and evil, but she was alive. She could

CHRISTINE DONOVAN

and would move on. She'd always possessed inner strength even if she didn't rely on it all the time.

For the past two months, she'd forgotten about her inner strength, but not anymore.

She lived.

She breathed.

She loved.

Her focus from this day forward was her husband and their marriage. Not the person who tried to destroy her. He didn't deserve even a moment's thought in her mind. Then she looked at her aunt and realized how devastated she was at the turn of events.

Miranda prayed every night for God to ease Violet's burden. Perhaps today was the answer to her prayers. No more wondering where the ne'er-do-well was. Had he taken the ship to America? Or was he strolling the streets of London?

They could breathe easy now knowing he would be on the next ship to New South Wales. Miranda should feel ashamed listening through the door after Spencer asked her and Auntie to leave, but, really, how could she walk away? She had needed to know what was happening even if she knew her husband would make things right. Which he did.

She still worried about Violet even though her aunt assured her she was fine. Perhaps it was time to put the past in the past and enjoy the present and look forward to the future. A future with the love of her life.

Just as she poured her second cup of tea the love of her life walked in the room commanding her attention. Not literally. Physically she was drawn to him. And it wasn't just his good looks, which he had in abundance, but his innate kindness and generous nature. She found herself smiling at him, hoping to relax him as he looked tense and stiff.

"Is he gone?"

"Yes. Smythe took him away. Neither of you will ever have to set eyes on the man again. He is as good as gone."

"Thank you," Violet said as she stood. "If you two don't mind, I think I'll rest before tonight's festivities."

"By all means." Spencer bowed. Once Auntie left the room, he shut the door and turned to her, looking concerned. "I am so sorry you had to see him again." Then he lessened the distance between them and pulled her into his strong arms.

"I'm not. It made me realize how fortunate I am to be alive. I have a second chance at life, and I plan on enjoying it as best I can."

"Music to my ears." Her eyes were riveted to his as the green took over the blue and darkened with lust and the gold flecks became more pronounced and he lowered his head and took her lips in a demanding kiss. He kissed her as though he would die if he didn't. As if he would wither and perish from thirst. They were married for a little more than a senight now, but she could count the number of times he kissed her like this on one hand. It was usually a soft, gentle meeting of lips. Not this tongue and teeth wet kiss that buckled her knees and had her hips pushing into him, seeking something beyond her grasp.

"Spencer." She broke away, leaned her head against his chest and breathed deeply until her lungs and heart resembled normal behavior.

"What my dear?"

"That nearly undid me."

He chuckled and the sound caused her skin to tingle. "I'm so very glad to hear it. Shall we rest before we need to dress for tonight's masquerade ball at my cousin's house? Now those are words I never thought I'd ever say before Amelia came into his life."

"Yes," she answered as her heart changed direction and began speeding up once more.

He took her hand in his warm, large one, and they walked side by side in companionable silence. Once inside their rooms, he pulled her into his arms again and looked deep into her soul, causing her to shiver.

"Whatever you want. I am yours to command. We will only do what makes you feel safe and good." His forehead came down to hers and rested there. "I'm nervous."

"*You* are nervous?"

"Yes. I don't ever want to cause you to worry. I love you too much. Witnessing your nightmares nearly kills me. Never, ever, do I want to see such fear on your face. You deserve everything that is good and kind and loving."

Her fingers curled around his waistcoat lapels and tugged his mouth down to hers. This time he waited for her to take the lead. She hesitated for only a moment then she swept her tongue inside his mouth and explored the way he did when he kissed her. The sliding of her tongue across his teeth and the moans vibrating in his throat had her rising on her tip-toes and devouring him.

"Easy darling," he said with a chuckle. "We are in no hurry." His actions contradicted his words as he unbuttoned his waistcoat, removed it, and tugged his shirt over his head leaving him naked from the waist up. Casually, he walked toward the bed, sat down and proceeded to pull off his boots.

CHAPTER THIRTEEN

MIRANDA COULD NOT HELP HERSELF FROM WHIMPERING when Spencer's hands went to the front placket of his pants. When his fingers stilled, she raised her eyes to his face and he grinned at her while his eyes twinkled with amusement. *The devil.*

"I believe you are overdressed." He rose, walked toward her, and she held her breath as his hands gently turned her around and he began the tedious task of unbuttoning her day dress. When her maid dressed and undressed her it seemed to be such a mundane part of her day. When Spencer unbuttoned each button, followed by his lips, kissing the exposed skin, she shivered and her head lolled back in utter bliss.

Time stood still. Good time. She was so lost in her blossoming arousal and enjoying her husband's hands and mouth on her, she barely realized when her clothing pooled around her feet and she was totally naked with his warm arms circling her waist.

"You are the most beautiful woman in the world." He released her and tugged her hand with his. "Come. I hear the bed calling our names."

Miranda was convinced she glided across the room because she didn't feel her feet touching the ground.

Right before her wide eyes, Spencer dropped his breeches to reveal his, large, hard, and pulsing manhood. For one moment in time she panicked at the sight of it, then she remembered he loved her and would never intentionally hurt her. He would die before he accomplished that.

As though he understood her silent concerns, he murmured, "Easy love. It's me. I will love and cherish you and no more."

"I know." Finding her courage she pulled down the coverlet and climbed on the bed, turned on her side, and immediately felt the dipping of the mattress as he joined her.

He reached out and skimmed his fingers up her arm, across her chest, and down the other side only to repeat the movement again. Each time the pads of his fingers touched her sensitized skin she quivered, closed her eyes, and sighed. He murmured sweet nothings in her ear. Comprehending the words he whispered didn't matter. What mattered was his tone. He spoke and touched her as if he cherished her.

When his warm lips replaced his fingers she moaned and silently hoped he never stopped touching and kissing her. Time became irrelevant as the room, the world and the universe collided and became one with them.

Her mind centered wholly on the touch and sounds coming from Spencer. He breathed heavily and moaned deeply. She sucked in her breath as his hand traveled down between her breasts, over the small swell of her stomach until it landed there. Slowly, ever so slowly, he moved his thumb in circles and her body answered. Her hips rose off the bed. When he removed his hand briefly she protested. "Spencer."

"I know darling. I know."

Then she gasped and her hips bucked up as his hot tongue licked her and his hands spread her thighs wide. His mouth sucked on her core and she didn't know what to do. Where to put her hands as the world exploded around her and she heard someone screaming and when Spencer climbed up her body and covered her mouth with his, the screams vanished and she realized they had come from her.

She should be mortified, but she didn't care. As his knee rose and he nudged her legs apart, positioning him over her, she waited for panic to come but it didn't. She wanted this. Wanted to know what it felt like to be loved completely by the man she cherished.

He entered her slowly, no doubt waiting for her to adjust. When it didn't happen quickly enough, she placed her hands on his hips, pulling him down until he was buried to the hilt inside her and all she felt was full. No pain, no anxiety. Comfortably full.

"Good?" Spencer asked looking at her with a worried expression. "Not moving is torturing me."

"Move. Please, move."

And move he did. Slowly at first then faster and harder and louder and louder they became until her insides tightened around him and she saws stars twinkling around the room. Spencer pushed one last time hard, froze, threw his head back and howled.

He collapsed on top of her, and she kept her arms and legs wrapped around his body, never wanting to let go. If she died tomorrow she would have no regrets.

Before she could stop herself she started to giggle. "I'm sorry. I was just remembering something my aunt told me her mother told her on the night before her wedding. How it was the wife's duty to close her eyes and think happy thoughts while her husband rutted between her legs. Who do you suppose made up such a ridiculous thing?"

"Some maiden who never married and experienced love-making. Or someone who married an elderly gentleman with no teeth, foul breath, and sagging skin."

She giggled once again. "What a horrible vision. I'll take my handsome, young, full rows of teeth and tight skin, husband any day."

"Do you mean it?"

"Oh," she moaned as his hands began exploring, followed by his mouth, and she clutched his upper arms ready for the wild ride to commence.

SPENCER COULD HARDLY BELIEVE the sight of his wife, lying naked, curled up against his side sleeping soundly after making love twice. He carefully, not wanting to wake her, reached down and pulled up the coverlet to keep them warm. If his sweaty body was chilled, she must be as well.

While he held the most precious person close to his heart, he relived the past hour and knew he had a stupid grin on his face. When he suggested they go up to their chamber he never really expected to consummate their marriage. Didn't believe Miranda was ready yet. Not after what transpired only hours ago.

Closing his eyes now, he swore he could still taste her sweetness on his tongue. The first time he sank his cock into her tight, warm channel he almost came instantly. It took all his self-control not to lose his seed. It was about her pleasure, not his. Only after she took hers, would he allow himself the privilege of his own release.

Nothing aroused him more than when she screamed to the point he had to kiss her to muffle her cries. Then, and only then, did he allow himself to come and enjoy his own release in his wife's delectable body. A body made for him. He fit perfectly inside her as he'd known he would.

During the second time, her body responded with even greater passion. He'd always known, when they first met all those years ago, that she was a sensual person. All he had to do was look into her eyes and the curiosity and lust that had been there at seventeen was still there at twenty-nine. Even more so. She was a woman now and had a woman's desires and needs.

Before he joined her in sleep, he wondered if they would make the masquerade ball at Bridgeton Manor later that evening.

"MIRANDA," Aunt Violet's voice came from the other side of the closed bed chamber door. "May I come in? We must leave for the masquerade ball in less than an hour, and I need your opinion on which mask to wear with my gown."

Both Miranda and Spencer sat up and realized they had fallen asleep.

"Please give me a moment and I will come to your room." Miranda turned to Spencer. "Go to your room and dress for tonight. I need to wash up and see to Auntie."

Spencer gave her a quick kiss on both cheeks and left through the adjoining door.

Miranda hurried into a dressing robe and walked briskly to her aunt's temporary chamber. Miranda would miss her terribly when she moved back into the townhouse on the outskirts of Mayfair. Once inside the room, she halted when she saw how beautiful and young Violet looked. "I love your interpretation of a Cyprian. I should be shocked, but somehow you pull it off without being overly exposed."

"Thank you, my dear. Although I do wonder how you know about Cyprian's and what they dress like." She held up two elaborate masks. "Which one do you think suits me best?"

"Try on the lavender, cream, and gold one. The colors bring out the cream and gold of your gown."

Violet put the mask on and Miranda clapped. "You look as young as a debutante."

"God, I hope not. I don't want to fend off young, handsome gentlemen all night long. But I would not mind finding a man close to my age to have an affair with."

Miranda inhaled and felt her cheeks heat.

"Don't look so shocked. I am but thirty-nine. I still have some good years left in me. I can never marry again, but I do like a man's attentions now and then."

"You are right. I should not be shocked. You are still young enough to...well...never mind. I've no doubt you will have all the eligible men close to your age vying for your attentions this evening."

Her aunt fluttered around the room, her cream silk gown flowing sensually around her, and Miranda only hoped her own costume looked half as good.

"Go now and dress. We don't want to arrive too fashionably late."

With Claudia's help, Miranda dressed as a gypsy. She and Spencer agreed to go as a gypsy husband and wife. When her maid put the finishing touches to her hair and make-up, Miranda stood in front of the cheval mirror and gawked at her reflection staring back at her.

She could not possibly be that person. Someone else stood there. Someone with strawberry-blonde hair hanging wavy and loose to her waist. The only adornment in her hair were red roses that matched her bright red full skirt. A white peasant blouse was tucked into the skirt and was accented with a wide belt in red, purple, and white. Her face was overly made up with red rouge and red lip color. Dark coal lines accented her eyes, making her look exotic.

No one would ever recognize her dressed like this, and she hadn't even put on her red sequined mask.

Before she had a chance to step away from the mirror, Spencer swept through the adjourning room and stopped dead in his tracks.

"Miranda?"

"Spencer?"

She barely found her voice to answer him. Never had she seen him look so handsome. Not in his formal clothes, nor dressed in his tight fitting riding clothes. The man before her looked dangerous and sexy and caused her heart to flutter and her body to tingle and heat up.

"Now I see why women find gypsy men so alluring." He was dressed in black tight breeches, polished black hessians, and a red blousy shirt with wide sleeves that tapered at the wrist and was scandalously open at the neck. The wide belt at his waist matched hers. His dark hair was slicked back off his forehead, except for one wayward curl. Her fingers itched to trace the stray lock.

"Miranda." Spencer's voice snapped her out of her thoughts. "Shall we leave or are you going to stare at me all night. Because if you keep at it." He grinned at her and his eyes narrowed sensually. "I won't be able to leave anytime soon." His hand gestured between his muscular thighs.

"Oh." She wondered if the rouge hid her blush. "I'm sorry."

The sound of her husband's laughter made her melt. "Never be sorry to look at me. I love when you do. And may I say, without offending you, that you look good enough to eat. I want nothing more than to find out what you have hidden beneath your skirts. Perhaps we should send our regrets to William and Amelia."

Now Miranda laughed. "Not a chance. I've never been to a masquerade ball and cannot wait to see all the costumes. Besides, I want to show off my handsome gypsy husband and make all the ladies jealous."

He held out his arm and with a wicked grin said, "Shall we, then?"

She wrapped her arm through his. "We shall."

Violet waited for them in the foyer and smiled when they came into view.

"Between the three of us we are sure to get the tongues of the *ton* wagging this evening. But then again, isn't the reason one attends a masquerade is so they can become someone else entirely. Even if that someone else is considered lower class and scandalous."

"Most definitely," Spencer agreed as he escorted both ladies to the carriage and before they knew it they arrived in the carriage queue at Bridgeton Manor.

Even though it was dark, Miranda pulled the curtain aside and peered out, soaking in the sights of all the colorful costumes people wore as they ascended the stairs. Before she knew it, she was alighting the brick staircase, Spencer standing between her and her aunt.

She couldn't help but wonder if there would be a regular receiving line where the butler announced their names. Her insides quivered. She didn't want people to know who she was until the midnight mask unveiling. She soon had her answer when they greeted their host and hostess without introductions. Miranda curtsied. "Earl, Countess, thank you for inviting us this evening." They were dressed as a king and queen. Which ones she did not know.

Bridgeton spoke up as he kissed her hand. "Welcome to our home." Then he winked. Of course he would recognize her. If not her, Spencer.

Spencer leaned in, spoke to Amelia and she smiled.

Next she was escorted into the ballroom on the arm of her husband with Aunt Violet trailing behind them and her steps faltered. The huge room was dimly lit, and she'd never seen such open flirtatious behavior before.

"Easy, my dear. Wouldn't want you tripping and falling on the floor. Not the entrance you were hoping for I'm certain."

"No. I'm just shocked. I feel as though we are attending a Cyprian's ball. Not that I've ever been to one, but I always imagined it would be like this. Dark and intimate with people standing close. Very close."

He chuckled. "Yes. That is the allure of masquerade balls. People can pretend to be who they are not. Or be the person they hide inside, behind the formal, starchy clothing and good manners. It is the reason most debutantes are not allowed to attend. If they were, can you imagine how many would be ruined because they were lured into the gardens by some wicked man?"

"I never thought of it that way. But you are right. This is no place for someone so young and innocent." She glanced behind her. "Aunt Violet disappeared. Do you think she will be safe on her own?"

"She will be fine. We are not actually at a Cyprian's ball. We are at William and Amelia's home. Nothing will happen to her here."

"I suppose you are right. She is a grown woman, married three times already."

"Exactly, my dear." He began walking. "I believe I see Wentworth and the rest of the Seabrook family over by the refreshment table. Shall we say hello?"

As Spencer led her across the room, she tried to figure out how he recognized the Seabrook family. There were so many people crowded in the room and all the colorful costumes and masks had her head spinning and her eyes straining to make out who people were. Not that she knew all that many people in London these days, since it had been many years since she attended a Season.

During her first Season, she'd attended balls, soirees, musicals the opera and the theater. Never a masquerade. Even though she attended many functions she could only remember Spencer, dancing with him and looking forward to his afternoon tea visits.

But this, this was something she never imagined attending and her insides hummed with excitement.

"Spencer, Miranda," Myles said as they approached.

"How on earth did you recognized us?" Spencer said.

"Easy. The same way you knew who we were."

After greetings were made the men sort off drifted off leaving the ladies to talk.

"Amelia dressed as a gypsy once during a masquerade at the Northborough Estate," Bella said. "Although I don't believe she looked as convincing as you do Miranda."

"Thank you. You and Myles look fabulous as Anthony and Cleopatra. Did Wentworth and Emma come?"

"No," Bella replied. "Emma was a little tired. Her time is coming close."

"How are you and Amelia feeling? One can hardly tell you are both increasing?"

"I can't speak for her, but I feel wonderful. No longer experiencing morning sickness. Myles is grateful for that. I never knew men had such queasy stomachs."

"I imagine he was worried about you."

"Yes, he was. Still is," Bella commented. "Tell me, how is married life to our dear Spencer?

Thankfully her rouge and mask hid her flushed cheeks. She knew Bella enough to know she hinted at their intimacy. Would she be shocked to know they only recently consummated their marriage? Probably. But not if she had knowledge of what occurred with Baker. Which made her wonder who knew from the Seabrook family and who didn't? Amelia and Bridgeton knew, but she didn't think anyone else did.

She didn't think even Amelia and Bridgeton knew what happened that morning when Baker arrived at their home. Unless at some point Spencer sent word to his cousin.

As she thought about her husband, he suddenly appeared at her side. "A waltz is beginning." He bowed and grinned. "May I have this dance, my fair gypsy lady?"

She curtsied and laughed. "Yes, my gypsy husband, you may."

Miranda hadn't danced in a very longtime and was a little apprehensive until Spencer took her into his arms, chasing her nerves away.

"I will never forget the first time we danced," he whispered in her ear.

"Nor I."

"Will you promise me you will never dance a waltz with another gentleman as long as I live?"

"I promise." Then he twirled her around the dance floor, her heart sang and her feet rarely reached the ground. Before she knew it, he danced her right out a set of French doors onto the veranda and escorted her into the dimly lit gardens.

They could still hear the orchestra. Spencer held her close and they swayed together, neither speaking. They didn't need to. Their bodies spoke for them. Never in all her life, had she imagined love could be so all encompassing. Nor, that she would ever see Spencer again, never mind marry him. The next time she saw her aunt she would thank her again for forcing her to come to London. She wished it had been under better circumstances though. Wishing they had come before her aunt's no-good husband stole everything from her.

If they had not come, she would still be living in the country, wandering around like a lost soul. Which was what she'd been doing for twelve years. Thankfully, not any longer.

"I can't believe we are married," she sighed as Spencer nibbled at her neck.

"Believe it." He nipped her earlobe with his teeth and she moaned. "We were meant to be together."

His lips sought hers and her body melted against him. Her lips parted, welcoming him, and all the sounds disappeared around her except for the pounding of her heart. He cradled her face with his hands and deepened the kiss. Then he broke apart, tore off both their masks and grabbed for her again.

"Better. Much better," he murmured as his lips traveled down her neck. His fingers tugged at the elastic neckline of her blouse, exposing her shoulder. His teeth skimmed across her newly exposed flesh and her knees almost buckled.

"Spencer," she cried as he tugged the blouse lower, exposing one breast to the cool night air.

"God. I can't get enough of you. Now that you're mine, I will never let you go. Never let you out of my sight. I love you so much it hurts at times."

Her head lolled back as his hot mouth sucked her nipple inside. "I don't want you to ever let me go. I'm yours for now and always."

One of his hands reached beneath her skirt and slowly, oh so slowly, slid up the inside of her leg until it found the opening in her pantaloons.

He exhaled loudly. "You're so wet. I wish I could make love to you here."

"As do I." Were those her words? When did she become so bold? Must be her new husband corrupting her with his sexual prose.

"We can't risk it, but I can..."

"Oh my God," she moaned as he inserted one long finger inside her while his thumb circled around her nub. "More."

She heard him chuckle against her chest. "Your wish is my command."

His talented fingers had her crashing over the edge of reality. She tried to be quiet, tried not to cry out. Thankfully, he knew enough to stifle her cries with his mouth as her body convulsed over and over until she thought she might fall to the ground in a heap of liquid. "Thank you," he murmured into her ear at the same time he dropped her skirt and righted her blouse.

"Should I not be thanking you?"

"No. Your pleasure is my pleasure. Hearing your moans of desire almost made me come in my breeches. Thank goodness I'm not eighteen, and I have some control over that appendage between my legs."

"Really," she teased as her hand drifted down and she cupped him. He squirmed away.

"Not that much control, my dear." He held out his hand. "Come. I do believe we need refreshments after that."

WHEN SPENCER first stepped into Miranda's room and saw her dressed in her gypsy costume he'd nearly dropped to the ground and wept. Never had he seen her look more enchanting, and he still couldn't believe they were married.

She was his. And he was hers. When his eyes had fallen on her, his body hummed with desire and he really didn't want to go out. All he wanted to do was strip off her enchanting and enticing clothing and bury himself deep inside her until neither of them could remember their names.

But he had an obligation to his cousin. If any other person was hosting tonight's masquerade he would have begged off. However, family was important to him. Besides, he wanted to show off his lovely bride. And keep an eye on his two sisters who would also be in attendance. Mary had two Season's already and Liz one, so Grandmother was allowing them to attend. Even though he fervently wished they were not.

He worried Liz might do something drastic to make Amesbury jealous and end up being on the front page of the scandal rags in the morning. Mary, well he didn't worry so much about her. She was timid and shy. But still, some less than honorable gentleman could take advantage of her good nature before she even knew what was happing.

Great, now his stomach pained with nerves. Until he looked at his wife again and all thoughts vacated his mind but getting to the ball and hurrying home so he could make love to her.

Aunt Violet was another sight to behold and he wondered what man would fall into her trap this evening. Because, without a doubt, she was dressed to seduce. She did deserve some happiness in her life after what Baker did to her.

Did to her and Miranda. *Don't think about it tonight?* He was gone and could never harm Miranda again. So he brushed it off and escorted two lovely ladies to the ball.

While he waltzed with his wife he quickly glanced around the room looking for his grandmother or his sisters. Perhaps they had changed their minds about attending. As long as they were not present, he could give all his attention to the woman in his arms. Half way through the waltz he had to escape. He had to get his hands on his wife. So he escorted her into the dark gardens and pleasured her. He could hardly believe she allowed him to lift her skirts and sink his fingers inside her warm heat.

Hearing her come apart, her hands digging into his arms, her heart pounding against his chest almost caused him to embarrass himself.

Just as he suggested they go inside for refreshments, they were rudely interrupted by a deep, masculine voice he didn't recognize...at first. When he did, it was too late.

CHAPTER FOURTEEN

Spencer moaned as he cradled his pounding head in his hands wondering why he was sprawled out on the hard ground in the dark with music playing in the distance. The smell of dirt, leaves, and flowers clung to his nostrils as well as something metallic.

When he removed his hands from his head, it registered in his aching mind, they were coated with something, warm, wet, and sticky. Blood. Blood gushed from the back of his head. Why? It took several tries for him to get his feet beneath his trembling body and when he did, the world spun in circles causing him to crash down onto his knees and vomit.

What the bloody hell happened to me? Where is Miranda? No. No. No. This can't be happening. I promised her I would keep her safe. Panic, fear, and anger forced the vertigo, nausea, and pain to take a holiday. This time when he stood, he focused everything he had on making it into William's house and seeking help.

He'd meant to enter into a private part of the house, but with his confused mind he entered the ballroom. Which was a good thing since his knees buckled and he hit the ground as soon as he made eye contact with William. Before darkness swallowed him, he believed he uttered the words "Miranda was taken." He could not be certain as pain exploded inside his head and he slid into a vortex of blackness.

"WHAT DO you suppose happened out in the gardens? And where is Miranda. Not to mention has anyone seen her aunt since she arrived?" William asked as he paced the confines of his study. It was like living his nightmare again when Amelia fell overboard on the Thames and Sir Phillip tried to drown her.

Sebastian, Myles, and Amesbury were present as they waited, none-too-patiently, for Smythe to arrive and hopefully shed light on the situation.

"I never saw the aunt and the last I saw Miranda she was waltzing with Spencer," Sebastian said in all seriousness as he downed a glass of brandy. "But in all truthfulness, Teagan and I were otherwise occupied."

"I didn't see the aunt either," replied Amesbury.

"Nor I," answered Myles.

"Does anyone know if Miranda or her aunt have enemies? Although, since they haven't been in town in many years, I don't see how?" This came from Myles who William, no doubt knew, was reliving his own nightmares when his cousin and his cousin's wife murdered his sister and tried to kill Bella and him by poison.

Due to the circumstances, William didn't believe Spencer would be upset if he confided what he knew to his friends. Hell, Smythe would be as soon as he arrived anyway. So he retold the story as Spencer had told him and three sets of eyes, full of concern and anguish met his.

"I know. It is a lot to accept. As far as I know, Smythe escorted Baker aboard a ship to New South Wales. Smythe is never remiss in his duties, but what other explanation do we have to their disappearance? Baker, somehow, got off the ship without Smythe knowing it. Damn." He raked his fingers through his hair in total frustration. "Spencer needs to wake-up, and soon. We need to know what happened. He must know something."

"Mr. Smythe," the butler said as he opened the door and ushered the haggard looking Runner inside and bowed out closing the door after him.

William handed Smythe a drink. "I think you're going to need this."

"Please don't tell me something has happened...again." Once his words were complete he downed his drink and held up his hand for another. "I've had a bad day and night. If you don't mind, I could use a refill." This time he took an empty chair and sipped.

Not that William always held to proper decorum, but he was surprised Smythe sat without being invited to. The man might be a Runner, but he had impeccable manners. Better than some members of the *ton*.

Tonight, however, Smythe looked exhausted and sloppily dressed. His eyes were glassy and sunk in his head with dark circles beneath them. Not to mention, he looked pale. For someone who spent much time in the outdoors, that was shocking to say the least.

"I'm ready now. Tell me what happened," Smythe said, followed by a sip of his drink with hands that trembled. *Bad day and night, indeed.*

"You're not going to like what I have to say. As you can tell by all the carriages and guests still milling about, Amelia and I hosted a masquerade ball this evening." William stood at a window, moved the curtain aside and stared into the very gardens where the crime took place. His insides quivered and he shook his head.

"Miranda and Spencer went out into the gardens. Sometime later, Spencer came back inside alone. He'd been hit on the head and knocked unconscious. I believe he muttered the words "Miranda was taken" before he passed out. He remains unconscious as we speak."

Smythe ran a shaky hand through his disheveled hair. "Damn."

"Miranda, as well as her aunt are missing," William said. "At least we think the aunt is. No one has seen her."

The look that crossed the Runner's features had William feeling sorry for him. He obviously believed this was his fault. As best as William could tell Smythe's age was somewhere around thirty. Tonight he looked decades older.

"I put the bastard on the ship. I even had men watching it until it set sail. The only thing I can come up with is once it left the dock he jumped ship. Crazy foolish thing to do. And so terribly bad for Lady Miranda and her aunt. How long ago did this all happen?"

"Best any of us can tell is about an hour from the time I sent for you."

"Do know where in the gardens it happened?"

"Hell, no," William growled. "When I get my hands on that bastard..."

"Easy. We all know that is not a good idea. Do you mind getting me a lantern and taking me into the gardens. I'm certain in the light of day, I could see better, but I don't want to wait."

By the time the men left the study, all the guests had departed and William sent Sebastian, Myles, and Amesbury to fill the women in on the situation. And to make sure someone came for him when Spencer woke up.

Smythe and William, each holding brightly lit, oil lanterns

entered the gardens. "He would have taken her to a secluded spot. Down one of the narrower paths, away from the lights glowing from the ballroom," William stated as he headed away from the veranda. "If I were looking for a little privacy I would head this way."

Smythe followed close behind as each swung his lantern side to side hoping to see something, anything that would clue them in to Miranda's disappearance.

"Here," Smythe said as he moved to the right. "Look at the crushed plants. Spencer had to have landed here." He hunkered down and ran his hand over the bent foliage and brought his fingers close to the lantern. "Blood. Which way to the street?"

"This way." William and Smythe followed a path they knew for sure Baker took Miranda through. The ground was disturbed and small flowers trampled. It led into the back of the property were the mews were.

They entered the mews and woke up the stable boy sleeping in a corner on a pallet.

"Did you see any strangers around here this evening?" William demanded.

The boy sat up, rubbed his eyes and then quickly stood. "Milord, there were several, but not unusual with the ball going on."

"Did you see a lady, being led away by a man against her will?"

The lad shook his head. "Didn't see no lady."

William told the lad to go back to sleep, and he and Smythe continued to look around. They wandered the streets of Mayfair and finally ended up back at Bridgeton Manor.

"You should go home." Smythe handed him his lantern. "I'll call in my best men and get right on it. Baker has no money, he cannot have gotten far with two reluctant ladies in tow."

William looked around for Smythe's horse. "How did you get here?"

"I took a hack."

"Well, there aren't any out at this ungodly hour. I'll send for my carriage and driver."

"No. I do my best thinking when I walk. Besides, it's only a couple of miles."

CHAPTER FIFTEEN

"MIRANDA, HONEY, WAKE UP. PLEASE WAKE UP." SHE HEARD her aunt's worried voice invading her ears and traveling into her mind, but her mind didn't want to work. It hurt too much. She truly didn't want to wake up. Nausea churned inside her stomach and pain stabbed her eyes when she opened them causing her to shut them immediately.

"No, you don't. Wake up. You need to wake up," her aunt's voice demanded.

"Why?" she managed to say.

"Because you have been unconscious for hours."

"Why?" And then she remembered watching Baker swing a club at Spencer. The sound of it hitting his skull, the way his body slumped toward the ground. She tried to help him but then she heard the crack of the club again and nothing.

"Ohmygod, Spencer. I think Baker killed him," she cried as her aunt hugged her and gently rocked her. It was then Miranda realized they sat on cold cement in a dark room smelling of mold and rotten dirt. Where were they?

"There, there, dear. I'm certain Spencer was hit just like

you and he will be fine. Right now he is probably scouring all of London looking for you."

"Yes, well, I don't know." She craned her neck looking for clues to their whereabouts. "Where are we?"

"I haven't the foggiest idea. The bastard waylaid me right after we arrived. I didn't recognize him in his costume until it was too late. He gagged and blindfolded me and snuck me out the servants' entrance. At least I think it was the servants' entrance. It doesn't really matter. What matters is he managed to kidnap both of us." She continued to rock. "I was angrier than anything at my stupidity in falling for his disguise when he brought me here. But when he came back with you...I'm so frightened for you."

"Spencer will come for us."

"That's my girl. Think positive."

Miranda was anything but positive. Her heart ached for her husband. Afraid for him. Afraid for her aunt and for herself. She didn't think she could live through Baker violating her body again.

As her aunt held her tightly, she surveyed her surroundings more closely. It appeared they were in some sort of jail cell. Perhaps a private residence. But who did Baker know in London that would help him commit kidnapping and allow him to keep his prisoners in their home.

"Did Baker have any friends or acquaintances in London?"

"None that I know of," Violet replied.

"Have you seen him since he brought me here?"

"No."

She rested her head on her aunt's shoulder. "My head throbs. You don't think he means to keep us down here, do you?"

"I hope not. But while we are here I need to confess something." Her aunt moved away just enough to take both of Miranda's hands in her icy ones. "I lied about having no money?"

Miranda went to pull her hands away, but Violet tightened her hold. "Lied? I don't understand?"

"I did what I did for you. Baker did take some money, but not all. I also didn't lose the house. I sold it. I couldn't let you continue living your life in the country. What if something happened to me, you would've been alone for the rest of your life."

Miranda rested her head back on her aunt's shoulder. It was too painful to continue holding her head up. "Thank you."

"Thank you?" Violet queried.

"If you weren't looking out for me I never would have married Spencer. So yes, thank you from the bottom of my heart."

"Even under the present circumstances?"

Before Miranda could respond, footsteps approached. "Hello ladies. Are your accommodations to your satisfaction because you will be here for the foreseeable future?"

"Why?"

"My dear wife, in case you haven't noticed, you and I are at war. You tried to send me to the Colonies." He visibly shivered. "And if that wasn't horrible enough, you then tried to send me to New South Wales of all places."

"You deserve no less for what you did to Miranda?" Violet screeched.

"Ah, so is that it? Are you jealous my dear wife? Because if you are, I can remedy that." He unlocked the door, closed it behind him and advanced on Miranda with a knife and rope.

"No," Violet screamed as she rushed towards Baker, who shoved her aside sending her crashing hard on the cement floor.

Miranda, eyes riveted to the steel in Baker's hand as he

advanced on her, backed up against the cold wall and tried to think of something to say to plead for her life. Impossible as her mind screamed inside her head wiping out any thoughts but the pain the knife would cause and the fact that she would never see the man she loved again.

"Easy, Miranda. Don't fight me. I'm only going to bind your arms and legs."

Relief washed through her body as she slid down the wall and sat with her legs and arms out in front.

Baker quickly tied her wrists together and then her legs. And to her shock, he tied her wrists and legs together making it impossible for her to stand. But why? They were locked inside the cell. Surely he didn't mean to leave her like that.

"Even if you scream, no one will hear you."

He turned and strolled menacingly across the cell to Auntie where he yanked her to her feet and touched the knife to her neck just enough for a drop of blood to slide down. Miranda swallowed her scream along with the bile rising up her throat. What did he mean to do?

"Be a good girl and I'll not need to use this again." He sheathed his knife into the waistband of his trousers. Grabbing the front of Violet's gossamer thin cream gown with his hands, he tore it from her body.

Who knew the sound of fabric tearing could be so deafening and painful to the ears.

Miranda didn't want to watch but was petrified to look away. In her mind, as long as she kept her eyes on her aunt, her aunt would be safe. Miranda was afraid if she looked away, Baker would kill her aunt. Take the terrifying sharp knife and slice through her neck.

Not rational thought, but nothing about this situation was rational. With her heart trying to leap out of her chest and her body trembling, she fought against her bindings. If only she could get loose she could snag his knife and turn the tables. He would be their prisoner. She would bury the knife so deep inside his chest, it would never dislodge.

To her dismay, all she managed to do was make the rough rope bite painfully into her skin.

The sound of her aunt begging her husband not to do this went unanswered. Seeing her aunt naked and vulnerable and being violated would haunt Miranda for the rest of her life. That was if she lived. Tears pooled in her eyes. Baker pushed Violet up against the wall, one hand holding both of hers over her head. With the other he exposed himself. Forcing her legs apart with his knee, he pushed into her aunt. A disgusting, inhuman sound fell from his lips, and Miranda shivered all the more.

She swore she lived it right along with her aunt. It was her aunt going through the rape, but Miranda saw herself in her place. Felt his vile hands on her body. His disgusting thing inside her. She closed her eyes tight. Could no longer look. The sounds were enough to have her gagging. Violet was silent and Miranda knew she would never cry out and give that bastard any opportunity to hurt her more. But the sound of him groaning and panting and the sound of their bodies slamming against each other had every muscle and tendon in her body screaming in pain. And her mind wishing for escape.

When at last there was silence, panic set in worse than before. Silence was more frightening because she didn't know what was happening, and she fought to open her eyes, but they refused.

The sound of footsteps moving her way had her cringing and waiting for her turn to come. For surely he intended to rape her as well.

He tugged at her bonds and the next thing she knew she was free. Inhaling deeply, she braced herself and opened her eyes.

It took a moment for her to register he was leaving.

Locking them in once again. She made quick work of hurrying to her aunt's side and covering her up with the remains of her tattered gown.

Lowering herself to the ground, she wrapped her arms around her aunt and rocked her like Violet had done to her not minutes ago.

Violet stared straight ahead as she moaned and rocked. Shock. She was in shock.

"It's going to be fine. He left. He won't hurt you again." Miranda didn't believe her own lies, but if they consoled her aunt, gave her peace and took her fear away, she would lie for all it was worth.

"Spencer will find us. I know it in my heart he will never stop looking for us." Of course it all depended on him being alive. A sharp pain stabbed her chest. *I will think positive. He is alive. I know it.*

"We just need to be strong for a while longer. Can you do that? Can you be strong?"

No answer. Miranda remembered how she was after her rape. She'd taken to her room, to her bed and stared endlessly at everything and nothing. Numb to all her surroundings. Broken inside. Damaged beyond repair.

Until one day her aunt had entered her room, flung open the drapes, ordered a bath and demanded she return to the living. She was not dead. It was time to heal her soul. Her body healed quickly, but her mind and soul still needed repairing and it was high time she started on the mending process. Hiding from life would not help her. She needed to face her demons and take back her life.

Her aunt saved her. Forced her to leave her room. Forced her to see that life still went on around her and she needed to join in. She was young and alive. Could not let that man destroy her life. If she didn't snap out of her shock, Baker won.

Having lived through what Violet just did, she knew it would take time for her aunt to heal. Only it was so much worse this time. He was her husband. He kidnapped them and imprisoned them. Did he feel any remorse?

Deep down inside Miranda feared he would be back to rape her. "Dear God," she prayed quietly. "Please don't let him come back. Please let us be rescued."

TENSION LIVED and breathed inside Bridgeton Manor twenty-four hours after the attack. Spencer could feel it trying to strangle him. He'd come to an hour ago, and since then his room had become crowded with all his family members.

He wished to hell they would leave him alone. His head pained him something awful, but that didn't compare to the ache inside his chest. Baker had Miranda. *His Miranda.* The thought of that man putting his hands on his wife had him seeing red. How he wished he could go back to the day the man arrived on his doorstep. Go back and kill him. England would be a much better place without the likes of him living within its borders.

Lying in bed, like an invalid, would never do. He didn't care that the physician said he had a skull fracture and needed to rest. The hell with that. Only, when he had tried to rise, the room spun, his stomach revolted, and white hot pain exploded inside his skull.

He never hated himself, ever, but right in this moment he despised himself for being weak. For succumbing to something beyond his control.

Trust. He had to place his trust in Smythe again. And William. He had to trust that they would find Miranda and her aunt and bring them home safe and unhurt. But, damn, his pride stung. It was his wife, it should be him out there hunting for her. Not lying here like the infirm.

And then his mind screamed. *Who cares who saves her as long as she is saved.* Damn his stubborn pride. He squinted around the room because it hurt to open his eyes fully. William, Amelia, Liz, Mary, and his grandmother stood around his bed.

"Stop staring at me, I'm not dying."

"You may not be dying now, but there was a moment when we feared you would," William said, looking somber and exhausted. Come to think of it, as he studied all the faces, they all had that in common.

"Did I really come that close to dying?"

His grandmother moved forward and took his hand. "Doctor Warren feared you might not recover consciousness. And if you did, you might not be yourself."

"Well, I can assure you, I am myself and I need to get out of this blasted bed." He exhaled and leaned back against the numerous pillows, frowning as he realized someone dressed him in a man's dressing gown. He'd never worn one in his entire life and couldn't believe where they unearthed one. He may, on occasion, don a dressing robe, but never a gown.

"Unfortunately, the pain in my head won't let me up. Tell me, what Smythe has found out. Because I'm assuming you sent for him, William."

"I did. The second you stumbled into the ballroom and collapsed. You caused quite a stir. One can only imagine what scandal is in the rags today. Not that any of us care." He rocked back on his heels. "As best as Smythe can tell, Baker must have jumped ship after it set sail. He'd had his men watching the docks the whole time until it left."

"That doesn't tell me anything about Miranda."

"He and his best men are scouring all of London looking for clues. Most likely he took them to the slums of London as

Baker had no money. Or he had an accomplice. Family nearby to help. Bloody hell."

"Bridgeton," his grandmother scolded.

"I beg your pardon. I'm just frustrated beyond proper speech."

"Has there been word?" Spencer asked as the room began to fade. He blinked his eyes, forcing himself to focus, but as William spoke again it sounded muffled, black spots flashed in and out of his eyes, and try as he might he couldn't fight the darkness swallowing him whole.

CHAPTER SIXTEEN

"HE'S OUT," AMELIA GASPED.

"The physician did say he could go in and out of consciousness for several days to come." William pulled his wife close and brushed his cheek against the top of her head. "It is probably for the best. There is nothing he can do, and I could see him struggling with being unable to help. Nothing is worse than being unable to help the one you love." William should know. He'd been unable to help Amelia when Sir Phillip had tried to drown her. And again when she regained consciousness and had lost her memory. Not being able to help had nearly done him in.

She hadn't known him. Her own husband. Wentworth had him thrown in Newgate believing he tried to kill Amelia. While he wallowed away inside a prison worse than hell itself, he berated himself because he didn't know what was happening outside. He didn't know what was wrong with Amelia. Even Spencer had a hard time finding out the truth. And if it wasn't for Spencer, he probably would have given up and succumbed to the madness trying to invade his mind.

Now he owed his cousin. He would do anything for

Spencer. Along with Smythe and the Runners, he was heading out shortly with Wentworth, Sebastian, Myles, and Amesbury. If Baker was still in London he would be found.

The alternative was too painful and frightening to consider. If they couldn't get Miranda and her aunt back soon, he feared for not only their lives, but Spencer's as well.

William knew all too completely what tragedy did to one's soul. He'd lived it for twelve years. Until Amelia.

Bridgeton waited downstairs in the drawing room for the men to arrive. He heard the door open and close, muffled voices, and turned from staring blindly out the window to find Smythe entering the room. His heart sped up with anticipation, then stopped dead away when he got a good look at Smythe's somber expression.

"I'm sorry, milord."

"We've been through enough together. Bridgeton, will do. And don't bow, for God's sake. I don't care about etiquette at a time like this."

"Bridgeton, I don't want to get your hopes up, but I think we've had a lead."

"Jesus, the way you looked when you walked in I thought you had bad news."

"Sorry. In my business I'm always serious." He combed his hands through his unruly, longer than customary, brown hair. "Some days I think I need a new line of work. I don't believe I've smiled in years. But never mind me." He shook his head, and William went to the sideboard to pour the fatigued man a whiskey.

"Perhaps this will help."

"Thank you. It's worth a try." He downed the liquid. "Damn that's mighty fine whiskey. I don't know if I'll ever be able to drink the stuff I have again." He placed his glass on the sideboard. "Do you mind if I sit."

"By all means."

William waited patiently as Smythe sat stiffly in a chair and sighed. "Thank you. Much better. As I was saying, we believe we have a lead."

"Not to interrupt. But what happened to you. I noticed last night you appeared injured. Are you?"

Smythe touched his side. "Knife wound. Don't worry, it won't keep me from doing my job."

"I'm not worried about that. You have never let any of us down. And when I say any of us, I mean my family and the Seabrooks. And I asked out of concern. Whether you have noticed or not, we see so much of you, I, at least think of you as a friend. I believe I speak for everyone else when I say that."

"You do," Wentworth said as he, Sebastian, Myles, and Amesbury entered the study.

"What happened?" Wentworth approached Smythe.

"He has a knife wound," William supplied.

"It happened two days ago. I'm fine."

William excused himself, left the room, and spoke to his butler. "Please fetch the physician."

"Actually, he just arrived and is with Mr. Spencer."

"Then tell him to come into the drawing room when he is finished."

Wentworth helped Smythe remove his coat exposing a white shirt coated in fresh blood.

"You are not fine. You're still bleeding and you look hot," William said. "The physician is with Spencer and will be down momentarily.

"That won't be necessary." Smythe went to stand, swayed, and sank back down into the chair. "Perhaps I do need a doctor. Thank you."

"No thanks necessary." William poured whiskey for the new arrivals and refilled a glass for Smythe who looked like he needed about four. He should have said something last night about being injured.

"How did it happen," Wentworth asked as he sipped his drink.

"One of my own Runners. Knew he was crooked as hell. Caught me off guard, which rarely ever happens. For his troubles he'll be buried in a pauper's grave."

"Good. I would hate to think you let him live after that," William said, feeling some satisfaction for the Runner.

"Hell no." Smythe downed his glass, leaned back. "We found out Baker has family in London. Believe it or not he is a distant relative of the Duke of Yarmouth." He paused and took a shallow breath. "We are watching his London residence. As soon as it's dark my men will get inside and search the place from top to bottom. If they are in there, they'll find them."

"The duke is depraved. If Baker went to him, he wouldn't care what he did to Miranda or Violet. He hates women if his treatment of Amelia was any indication."

"I know. And that's what troubles me." Smythe's speech sounded slurred. On two drinks? Now William was truly worried. He'd seen the man drink much more than that and not feel any effects of the alcohol.

The butler announced the doctor. "This good man has been stabbed. He needs care," William stated.

The physician spoke quietly to Smythe, then removed the man's shirt and Smythe hissed as it was pulled over his head revealing a cloth bandage wrapped around his midsection stained with old and new blood. It was then William's nose detected the stench of infection. He glanced at his companions and saw they all noticed as well.

"The wound is infected. He needs medicine and rest," the doctor said as he rummaged inside his medical bag.

William left and reentered. "The housekeeper is preparing a room. Let's get you up."

"No. I can't ppppossibly impose."

"You can and will." William and Wentworth each took a side and helped Smythe stand. William noticed right off how hot his skin was to the touch. He'd always admired Smythe, but he did even more so now. The man would've hunted for Miranda and Violet at risk to his own life.

After getting him settled in a room, the doctor made them all leave. A short time later he entered the hall to concerned looks on all the men. "I cleaned his wound, rewrapped it, and gave him laudanum to ease the pain and help him sleep. I think we caught the infection in time. But only time will tell. I will be back on the morrow to look in on both Mr. Spencer and Mr. Smythe. Good day. I can see myself out." The middle-aged doctor walked down the hall carrying his carpet bag of medicines and instruments.

"What do we do now?" Sebastian asked.

"You may as well go back to your wives. Smythe's men will contact me when they find out anything more. Let us pray Miranda and Violet are at the duke's residence. That way, they should be home tonight." Once alone, William paced the small room, hoping to exhaust his mind and body enough so he could relax.

"May I come in?"

"Always," he replied with a smile and zing to his heart. When he opened his arms, she walked right in, resting her head on his chest and wrapping her arms around his waist.

"You look tired. You haven't slept since before the ball. Come. I'll tuck you in."

William rested his cheek on the top of her head and inhaled her lavender scent. The same scent he smelled the first time they met. It would always remind him of her.

"That sounds wonderful, but what if Spencer or Smythe need me."

"Smythe?"

He proceeded to explain about the Runner.

"Oh dear. The poor man. We owe him so much already. It's the least we can do. I'll check on him when you are settled in bed.

"Have Mary or Liz. I want you to myself."

"Your wish is my command."

WHEN SMYTHE CAME AWAKE he looked around, and his investigator's mind came to several conclusions. The sun had set and he had no idea where he was. He kicked off his covers as he'd broken out in a sweat. Knife wound. Infection. Fever. He was in the house of the Earl of Bridgeton.

The other thing he noticed was a lovely young lady sitting in a chair dozing. He had seen her before, even though they were never formally introduced. She was one of Mr. Spencer's sisters. Which one he did not know.

As her head bobbed forward he studied her features illuminated by the candle light. Her hair was a pale blonde, her lashes slightly darker as they rested against her skin. He wondered if her eyes were blue or green. She looked slight of frame. Although she had curves. Her wrap failed to hide the swells of her breasts over the scooped neckline of her light pink dress.

What was she doing in here? If anyone found out she would be ruined. Spencer would kill him. He would not want a Runner for a brother-in-law.

"Excuse me miss," he said in a voice he hardly recognized. "You need to wake up."

She lifted her head, locked eyes with his, and smiled as she raised her arms over her head to stretch. "You're awake. How do you feel?"

He died. There was no other explanation for this angel sitting at his bedside. Blue. Her eyes were a strikingly deep blue. Suddenly, he had difficulty getting air into his lungs.

"Who are you?"

"I'm sorry." Even in the candle light he witnessed her blush. "I'm Mary. Spencer's sister. I was afraid you might wake-up in the night and need assistance. My sister, Liz, is sitting with Spencer. So I thought..." She shrugged her shoulders. "I would keep watch on our other patient."

"You need to leave." The moment the words left his mouth, he regretted the harshness of them, and his stomach twisted up around the knife wound at the hurt look that replaced the happy one from moments ago.

"Forgive me that was harsh." He pulled the covers up over his chest, which he just realized was naked except for the bandage. "I mean. It's not proper for you to be in a room alone with an unmarried man."

She waved her hand around. "Oh, that. Nonsense. I'm playing nurse and you're my patient."

Damn if his blood didn't pump southward. She was adorable and so innocent. She had no idea what she insinuated. He needed to tread very carefully around her.

"I thank you for looking over me while I rested."

"Oh." Her smile faulted again.

"What I mean to say is, you must be tired and in need of rest yourself. I feel much improved." And then he remember his case. "Do you know if any of my men came by this evening?"

Her smile came back brighter than before, if that were possible. "Yes. That is another reason why I came in here. If you woke up I wanted to give you the good news. Your men rescued Miranda and Aunt Violet."

Suddenly, exhausted beyond reason, he sighed and thanked Mary. At least he thought he said the words before he drifted into a hazy sleep.

CHAPTER SEVENTEEN

Not long after Baker raped Aunt Violet, he came back to leave a pitcher of water and some stale bread. The small loaf would likely break a tooth if they ate it, it was so hard. But the water was a welcome respite. Miranda held the pitcher for her aunt, encouraging her to drink. After she took a sip, Miranda did as well then hugged her aunt close again hoping to ward off the chill and to ease her aunt's burden and pain.

Miranda must have dosed off because she started awake at the sound of someone whispering her name in the dark. "Here," she whispered back as she struggled to stand. "I'm here."

"Bow Street Runners here to take you home."

"It's locked."

"Do not fret, milady. I have the key. As the man got closer with his lantern, she realized there were two men, not one, and they were young and dressed completely in black.

"Quickly before Baker returns."

"He's dead, milady. There is nobody here but the duke's servants and they are frightened."

Air expelled from her lungs and she nearly collapsed to the ground in relief. They were safe. Baker could never rape either of them again. As the men entered the cell she asked, "Can either of you gentlemen lend me your coat for my aunt?"

The smaller of the two didn't hesitate before he shrugged out of his overcoat and handed it to her.

"Thank you, kindly."

Miranda pivoted around and hurried to her aunt who still sat on the cold, damp floor staring into nothing. Miranda's heart sank at the lost look on her face. How would she ever make it right for her?

"Aunt Violet," Miranda said in a soft voice as though she were talking to a young child. "These men have come to take us home. Here, I have a coat for you to keep you warm."

When she helped her aunt stand, her gown gaped open. Miranda quickly pulled it closed and slid her arms into the coat and buttoned it up. She rolled up the overly-long sleeves and wrapped her arm around Violet's waist. Silently, they followed the men down a hallway and up a rickety set of stairs and into an opulent home lit by several candles casting shadows eerily on the walls, floor, and ceilings.

Miranda fought the urge to flee from this unwelcome home. She needed the safety of the outdoors. Craved fresh air. Instead, she forced herself to continue walking slowly, helping her aunt along. When they descended the outside stairs and came face to face with a carriage baring the Earl of Bridgeton's crest, she breathed a deep sigh of relief. Because for the first time since she found herself in Baker's company, she believed everything would turn out fine.

After she was home and back into Spencer's safe arms, she would find a way to help her aunt heal.

The coach ride was the longest in her life. She sat with Violet wrapped in her arms and her head resting on her shoulder. The two Runners sat opposite, neither looking at them, and she appreciated their privacy. The last thing she needed was strangers watching. If she saw pity in their eyes her defenses would come crashing down and she'd be useless to Auntie.

When the wheels came to rest, Miranda closed her eyes and said a silent prayer to God. *Please let my husband be alive and well. I cannot fathom life without him.* And she couldn't. They may have only recently been reacquainted, but he was her everything. Her heart, body, and soul belonged to him. Completely and desperately. The urge to crash through the unopened carriage door, run up the stairs and into the house screaming his name was hard to fight.

Someone needed her. The person who had been there for her since her parents' deaths. The person who brought her back from the brink of wanting to die. Made her travel to London and find the man of her heart.

"Auntie," she crooned. "We are back at Spencer House." Only when the door opened, she realized they weren't home. They were at Bridgeton's. It didn't matter, it was as good as being home. "We are at the Earl of Bridgeton's home." One of the Runner's helped her down the steps, she turned and held out her hand to her aunt. "Come. Let's get you a nice hot bath and tucked into a warm bed."

The look in her aunt's eyes, had tears pooling in hers. She resembled a simpleton. "Please. It is safe here."

She reached farther into the carriage, and finally her aunt placed her hand in hers and let herself be led from the vehicle. Before they had a chance to ascend the steps, Bridgeton, the butler, and housekeeper met them.

The relief on Bridgeton's face was short-lived when he looked at Violet and then her.

"My aunt needs care. I will explain all later." Without saying a word, the housekeeper gently wrapped an arm around her aunt's shoulder, spoke quietly to her, and led her inside the house.

Once she no longer had a reason to be strong, her body began vibrating, her teeth chattered, and tears rained down her face, followed by heart wrenching sobs. And that wasn't the worst of it. She bent over and cast up her accounts, splattering the earl's boots.

"I'm so sorry."

"No need." Before she could protest he swept her into his arms, ascended the steps into the foyer, and continued up the grand staircase, down a hall, and kicked open a door to a dark chamber.

"Do you think you can stand for a moment while I light a candle and stir the embers?"

"Yes." When he put her down, she locked her knees to keep herself from dropping like a marionette doll with its strings cut.

Once the candle was lit and flames glowed in the hearth, her eyes rested on the pale man with a white bandage wrapped around his head lying on his back in a large four poster bed.

"Oh God," she cried as she hurried to the bedside, her melt-down of moments ago vanishing as panic took over at seeing Spencer looking so ill.

"What did the physician say?" *Please let it be good news*.

"That he has a fractured skull and needs to rest. If he could have hunted down Baker and rescued you himself he would have. But damn it, each and every time he tried to get up he vomited and passed out."

"He hit me as well. But obviously not as hard. No doubt he meant to kill Spencer but not me."

"Indeed. He is lucky to be alive. But not just alive. Alive with all his facilities."

Her hands reached out, resting on the bed for support.

"Amelia's ladies' maid should be in any moment to help you clean up. I think it would do wonders for my cousin if he woke up with his wife beside him."

"Thank you."

After the maid helped her wash most of the grime from her body and hair, she dressed in a clean night rail and climbed underneath the covers, curling up against Spencer. Even though he slept, he sighed and moved closer to her body as if he knew she was there.

CHAPTER EIGHTEEN

Warmth woke Spencer out of a deep sleep which had brought him relief from pain. The right side of his body was overheated and something was tickling his face and chest. Before he dared open his eyes, because the past few days brought him nothing but excruciating pain when he did, he reached for his face and came in contact with soft, silky hair.

His eyes popped open, and he saw his beautiful wife curled up against his side. The stabbing pain inside his skull eased.

He didn't move, afraid to wake her because he wanted to enjoy this moment. He wanted to study and memorize every single part of her. It wasn't easy as his heart throbbed inside his chest causing his whole body to vibrate. He so desperately wanted to touch her. Love her. But he didn't want to be greedy.

After the ordeal she went through, she needed her rest. It took restraint not to wake her up so he could be reassure she went unharmed. Unviolated by that man. But the answers could wait. Meanwhile, he would close his eyes and revel in the knowledge he had Miranda back.

Nothing or no one would ever take her from him again.

"Are you awake?"

Her voice traveled inside his body and curled around his heart. "Yes. Welcome home."

"I'm so sorry about what happened. If I hadn't married you, you would not be in bed with a head injury."

Fighting through the pain throbbing inside his skull, he turned onto his side and looked into her worried, soft green eyes. "I would do anything for you. Die for you. Fight for you. Because my life is nothing without you in it. Haven't you figured that out by now?"

Tears leaked from her eyes and he gently wiped them away with his fingertips. "When I was locked inside that cell I thought I'd never see you again. That if I somehow managed to escape, you would be dead. I thought he killed you."

"Oh, my dear, it takes more than the likes of Baker to put me in the ground."

"He is dead."

"Good." And afraid to ask, but needing to know, he said, "Did he..."

"No. But it was horrible." She buried her face into his neck. "He raped Aunt Violet right in front of me." She inhaled deeply, and he could feel her heart pounding rapidly against his side. "He tied me up. There was nothing I could do. I feel so guilty that I made it out unscathed."

"Thank God you did. How is Violet?"

Sobs caused her body to tremble from head to toe. "Ever since it happened she has stared at nothing, said nothing. Appears like a child. I'm afraid I've lost her for good."

"I will hire the best doctors. We will not rest until she is recovered and herself again."

"From experience, she will never be the same."

"I realize that, but look at you? How far you have come.

You will be her best advocate. She is a strong woman, I believe she will eventually recover. It may take days, perhaps months, but she will crawl out of her own internal nightmare and come back to us. What other choice do we have? Give up and let her wallow until death takes her?"

"Thank you."

"For what?"

"For saying the words I needed to hear right now." Her chest pushed against his side as she inhaled and exhaled. "The whole time it was happening, I relived my violation. I nearly descended into the darkness with her."

"Never again sweetheart. The man is dead and can never hurt you or your aunt again. And as long as I'm alive no one else ever will. Now rest. It's still early and to be honest, I need to close my eyes to ease the pain inside my head. Will you stay with me?"

"There is nowhere else I'd rather be. I love you."

"I love you, too."

LATER THAT DAY Smythe came to visit Spencer, and Spencer thought the Runner looked worse than he did. "What happened to you?"

"Never mind me. I'm sorry. I failed you."

"Nonsense. It's not your fault. All that matters is that Baker is dead. Miranda is fine and I'm convinced her aunt will be in time."

"But still. Doesn't sit well in my gut."

"Your men found them. Rescued them and killed the bastard. *Your* men. Under *your* orders. You did your job and did it well. Sit, you look ready to collapse."

"No. I must be getting home. Please express my gratitude to the earl." Halfway out the door, he turned and exhaled. "I hope to hell I don't see any of you anytime soon. Except in a social situation."

MIRANDA WAS anxious to get home, but unfortunately, Spencer needed another day or two to recover. And as far as her aunt went, it probably wasn't a good time to move her either. Even though she did nothing but sit in a lounge chair by the hearth in her room, she seemed content.

If only her aunt would look at her with something other than emotionless eyes. Seeing her that way was worse than terrible. Gone was the exuberant and happy aunt she knew and loved, and it tore at her insides.

When would she come back? The physician said her mind was protecting her from what she went through. When she was ready to face it, she would. But in the meantime, she was to be treated with care, but under no circumstances should she be ignored. Treat her normally and perhaps she would recover sooner rather than later.

So Miranda sat in a chair, next to her aunt, who reclined on a lounge chair, and told her about her day. And how tomorrow they hoped to move back home.

Perhaps if the weather fared well, they could ride in the park. On and on Miranda went, making small talk, hoping and praying to hear her aunt's voice speak back. Her shoulders slumped when all that reached her ears was silence. She would not give up. In her heart she had to believe that eventually she would come around. Baker would not win.

IT TURNED out to be two days later when Spencer, Miranda, and Aunt Violet moved home to a big welcome from Liz,

Mary, Spencer's mother and grandmother. Never had she felt so drained of energy. If it wasn't for her husband giving her confidence about her aunt's recovery she would give up.

After getting Violet settled inside the room she was staying in, she sought the comfort of her bed, planning to rest her weary mind and spirit. Claudia helped her undress down to her chemise and tucked her in. As tired as she was, she couldn't manage to close off her mind long enough to allow sleep to come. Just when she decided to give up on napping, Spencer entered the room.

"Are you feeling unwell?" The caring in his voice turned her stomach to mush.

"No. Tired is all. How do you feel?"

"The pain in my head has finally dissipated, and I feel like a new man."

He certainly did if the twinkle in his eyes was any indication.

"I thought I would join you, spend some time holding my wife." As he undressed, her eyes were riveted on him. She never imagined a man's body could be so beautiful. A contrast between soft and hard. Once, unabashedly naked, he pulled the covers back, climbed in the bed beside her and turned so they were face to face.

"Miranda. If you are not up to this, please let me know." His eyes searched hers, his confidence from moments ago wavering. "I don't care if for the rest of our lives all we do is hold one another close. Being with you in any capacity is better than not being with you at all. I have to tell you though, when I came to and found out Baker had you, part of me died inside at the thought of never seeing you again. Never being about to tell you how much I love you."

"When I was locked in the cell, I was afraid you were dead. My heart tried to tell me you were alive, but my mind wouldn't listen. My one regret was you. Not having had enough time with you to express my love and devotion. Never have I ever loved another. I've loved you for so long, you feel a part of me. You're inside my heart, my body, my soul. And don't believe for one moment I don't want this. This joining of our bodies. Joining of two hearts into one."

She reached out her hand and placed it on his cheek. "I love you so much. It used to hurt to love you when we were apart. But not anymore. Because loving you has healed my broken heart. Love me Spencer. Love me with your body and your heart."

When he reached for her she breathed a deep sigh of relief, knowing their future looked bright. "Shall we try for your heir?"

"If you insist."

"I do."

As he brought his lips to hers, she forgot about being tired or stressed. Being in Spencer's arms, being cherished and loved by him caused the rest of the world to vanish. Nothing mattered but the two of them and the love they shared and the future that was theirs.

ABOUT THE AUTHOR

Christine Donovan is an International Bestselling Author and PAN member of RWA. She belongs to NINC and Rhode Island Romance Writers. She lives on the southeast coast of Massachusetts with her husband. She has four grown sons and one granddaughter. When she is not writing or reading, she is either painting or gardening.

Visit her at **http://www.christinedonovan.org**
or email her at **christinedonovan6@verizon.net**

www.ingramcontent.com/pod-product-compliance
Lightning Source LLC
Chambersburg PA
CBHW032138170626
46808CB00006B/2293